THUNDER STORM

MIMI FOSTER

THUNDER STORM
Copyright © 2014 by Mimi Foster
Published by *Feith Press*

ISBN: 9780989705394
ASIN: B00L88VHT6

Cover design by The Killion Group http://thekilliongroupinc.com

This book is dedicated to my mother,

Virginia Elizabeth Jordan Henry

1920 - 2014

My biggest fan and inspiration

CHAPTER ONE

It wasn't fair she should be the one being buried. Even the skies mourned and wept with us. The drizzle turned to sleet as the black cars snaked their way through the streets of Brooklyn. The sun had not made an appearance in days, adding another layer to the dreamlike quality of the past week. The clouds that were now low enough to weave their tentacles around the slow-moving procession were closing in like the reality of her death.

"I'll come see you tonight, I promise," I had told her. "I'm sorry I haven't been there this week, but landing this new client has been a year in the making. It'll rocket my little advertising agency into the stratosphere. This is what I've been working so hard for, and it's starting to pay off."

She'd been so pleased for me and couldn't wait to hear. But I didn't make it that night. A last-minute phone conference from the new client had lasted almost two hours. Repeated calls to explain my absence went unanswered. It was so unlike her, but I presumed they were doing their nighttime routine. I was genuinely concerned the following morning hearing the monotonous echo of unheeded calls. I took an extended lunch to check on them.

The front door was locked, and no one answered the bell. I used my key. "Mama? You here?" The dishes were stacked neatly in the drainer on the counter. "Mama?" I opened her bedroom door. They were both in her bed.

"Mama!" I cried, seeing her lifeless body in the arms of the woman who had given her birth. I wanted to back away, not comprehending that my vital mother could be dead.

"She's so cold," said my grandmother. "I thought I could warm her if I held her."

"Oh, Mama!" I dissolved into tears, kneeling by the bed, my head on her chest, sobbing uncontrollably.

"Hush, now. You're gonna wake her, and she's so tired. Hasn't moved all morning."

"Nana, come with me, darling. Please, let's leave her to rest for a while." I wept as I helped her out of bed.

"Jeni's gonna be here soon. She'll know what to do."

I called the coroner's office.

"Who *are* you?" my grandmother asked.

"I've come to help you. Let's get you dressed, sweetheart, before the men show up."

Shards of ice cut across the glassy rooftop of the limousine, mirroring the three saddest days of my existence. I pressed my chest as we left the cemetery, trying to relieve the pain. I wouldn't have made it without Jordan and her matter-of-fact attitude.

"What's the immediate plan? I'll stay for the week and do as much as I can to help out." She rubbed my frozen fingers.

"I appreciate that, but what about Brandan? Won't he be upset with his bride being gone so long?"

"He's recovering well and getting stronger every day. He knows how important it is that you're not alone right now. Relax and let me be here for you like you always are for me."

"How will I ever be able to thank you?"

"I would have fallen apart if you hadn't been there for me after his accident. I'll help get things settled as much as possible before I head back." She tucked another tissue in my hand.

"I can't believe she's dead. It was so sudden, so unexpected, and I break down every time I think of her."

"Give it some time. It's only been a few days."

"Guilt is getting the best of me on so many levels," I said, touching the necklace she'd given me long ago. "I wasn't there for her that last week, and she never mentioned anything about not feeling well."

"You had absolutely no way of knowing."

"Poor Nana. The only person she recognized is suddenly taken from her, and I landed an ad campaign for a national client I've been courting for over a year. I feel callous and selfish for trying to figure out how fast I can get back to work, if for no other reason than to not be alone with my thoughts."

"Then we'll keep her nurse for another few days, and you'll go back to work tomorrow." Years of being a sharp New York lawyer reflected in her take-charge approach, but her recent life running a charming Bed and Breakfast in an obscure Colorado town had softened the edges. "I'll interview the top five facilities that take patients with her issues, and I'll give you the material to make an informed decision."

"There's no way . . ."

"There's no argument. It's done. If you think you can face it, you're going back tomorrow."

"What would I do without you, Jord? Do you know what an answer to prayer you are?"

"I'm still trying to wrap my brain around all this myself. I can't imagine what you're going through."

The rain slowed as we arrived at the funeral home. Rays of sunshine peeked from behind bleak clouds. "It's going to get better, darling, I promise."

There was a sense of panic as Jordan gathered the last of her things from my apartment before the taxi arrived. "It would've been so much worse if you hadn't been here. Nana was dreadfully confused those first few days with everything changing around her so quickly. She seems to be settling into the nursing home, but I'll never be able to thank you for sharing your strength with me."

"Are you kidding? You've taught me everything I know about sharing strength. It's what friends do."

"Even so, you've been a lifeline, and I'll be forever in your debt."

"Listen," she said, taking on a serious tone. "You're not alone. You know you can come stay in the cottage any time. I told you, if you ever need to change things up, we'll find a nurse and you and Nana can stay there for as little or as long as you need. Besides, Miles is always asking about you, so it's not like there's not a gorgeous reason to visit."

"I appreciate your offer, you know I do, but things are insanely busy here and I'm not sure I'm gonna have time to even breathe. By the grace of God, Nana's close enough I'll be able to stop by there often. And are you *nuts*? Talk about distractions I don't need in my life – Miles makes me forget even my own name."

"Yeah, he's got your number, that's for sure. But when he mentioned your green eyes the other day, I figured he had it just as bad as you do." She laughed at my stunned expression, then hugged me. "Don't forget to take care of yourself, Jeni. None of this is worth it if you collapse from exhaustion."

I thought about her words over the next few weeks as one day bled into another. When I considered the possibility of taking Nana to Colorado, I often wondered if part of my judgment was clouded with a selfish desire to see Miles again.

Miles Jeffries, a business partner of Jordan's husband, Brandan, was a perfect specimen of a human. We'd met a few times at Jordan's Bed and Breakfast and were attuned enough to each other that I found him hard to forget, as much for his kindness as his good looks. Over six feet tall, handsome, buff, compassionate, short dark hair and eyes the color of a tiger's, he was a complication I didn't need in my life. But I was honest enough with myself to admit I didn't mind fantasizing about him occasionally. He was a pleasant distraction from my everyday routine.

In the meantime, I fit in a visit to Nana every day or two. Sometimes she knew me, sometimes I was a nice young lady who stopped to visit. The times that were the hardest were when she thought I was my mother. "Oh, Janet, I'm so glad to see you," she said that afternoon. "Let me get my coat and I'll be ready to go."

"We're not able to leave yet. Maybe tomorrow," I said quietly.

"I don't want to be here anymore. It's time to go home. You said they were coming to get me. Where are they?" She was agitated.

"I'm so sorry, they had to cancel for today. Maybe we can go tomorrow," I improvised, hoping she'd forget by then.

"Why didn't you tell me? I've been waiting all afternoon."

"I just found out myself. I'm sorry. But I'll stay with you."

"I don't want you to stay with me, I want to go home." Her voice grew louder. The nurse asked me to leave. I blamed myself as I walked the long city blocks to my co-op.

My small but eager staff worked with me to keep up with the influx of new accounts. My business was prospering, the payoff from all I'd struggled so hard to achieve. Twelve-hour days weren't enough to keep up with the demand.

When I slowed down enough to become conscious of life around me, I'd slam the lid on the nagging doubts of why I was working this hard, especially since the only thing I ever truly felt anymore was exhaustion. I'd spent years getting here, neglected family and friends to make a name for myself, so it had to mean something, right? The alternative was too overwhelming to face.

When my treasured assistant, Claire, went into labor toward the end of her seventh month of pregnancy, it was a blow to the smooth flow of business when she told me she wouldn't be coming back. She said the life she'd borne was too precious and still too fragile to leave in daycare.

Days blurred, deadlines were met in the final minutes, and often I'd stop to see Nana. Each time I grew more concerned with her lethargic state. Spare time wasn't something I owned, and I didn't know what the solutions were. When I allowed myself to feel anything, my conscience whispered to me of neglect.

"Ms. Jenkins?"

"Yes, this is Jeni."

"This is Leigh Ann from Goodfellow Nursing Home. We're sorry to inform you that your grandmother walked out of an unlocked door this afternoon. We're doing everything we can to find her, and will keep you updated on our progress."

Hours passed. I was distracted from my project and called every half hour to see if there were updates. Unable to concentrate, I arrived at the nursing home as one of the administrators stepped out of a police car, escorting Nana to the door.

"Oh, here's my daughter now," she said. "She can take me home."

"Where did you find her?" I was relieved she wasn't wandering aimlessly.

"She was about a mile away at Tom's Tavern having drinks with some of the locals. When she started undressing," the officer said with a sympathetic smile, "the bartender understood something wasn't quite right and called us."

"No! I don't want to go in there! I want to go home!" she was shouting in the doorway. "Please, Janet, take me home! I don't want to come back here!" She was trying to break loose, and several of the staff came to help get her inside.

"Janet, *please*!" she cried. "*Please*, take me home."

"Thanks for bringing her back," I said, tears flowing freely. I was crushed as I followed them inside and helped settle her into bed.

"Don't make me stay here," she begged, smelling strongly of alcohol as she drifted to sleep. I held her hand for a while, achingly conflicted.

When I showed up the next evening, she was comatose. In response to my questioning, the nurse explained they often increase the dosage of medications on patients who run away to help calm them. It made me physically ill.

I called Jordan as I walked home that night. "I'm so lost." I was as close to defeated as I'd ever been.

"Tell me what's going on," she said in her no-nonsense tone that always helped me gain perspective.

"I can't seem to balance it all anymore. I keep wondering why I'm working this hard." I told her about Nana, about her running away and how she seemed to be deteriorating. I told her about work and being too busy to even hire more staff, and that my purpose for doing what I was doing seemed to be shrouded. And I told her how much my heart hurt, and that I broke down and cried at odd times.

She listened sympathetically, and when my tearful enumeration was complete, she asked, "What do *you* want to do?"

"I want her out of there, Jord. I'm not sure what to do, but I know I can't leave her there. I vacillate between guilt, love, resentment, love, frustration.

Everyday I'm aware I'm distracted, but don't know how to give it my full attention."

"Do you want to bring her to Madeline Manor? She loved it here, we can get her a full-time nurse and let them live in the cottage. Miles and Brandan have already started with the repairs so it'll be finished whenever you're ready to take that leap."

"Really?"

"Yeah. Brandan's working on it because we've been talking about finishing it since the main house was done. Miles offered to help. I'm sure a lot of his motivation was to encourage your decision to fall on the Colorado side of the fence."

"Good grief — words that come to mind when I think of Miles — sexy as hell, temptation, unavailable, complication."

"Do you really think he's unavailable?"

"Not gonna happen. He makes my toes curl just thinking about him, but he's there and I'm here, and he's made it crystal clear he's not interested in a short-term, long-distance relationship."

"I don't know. You guys had some pretty spectacular chemistry."

"Thanks, but no thanks. No room in my life for any kind of diversion right now, especially one that turns my brain to mush."

"Well, think about sending Nana out here, at least. I may be familiar to her, and I'm around enough I can oversee her care each day. That may release *some* of the burden from you."

"My mom, bless her heart, left a hefty life insurance policy that'll let me take good care of her, so we can afford private nursing. Let me sleep on it for a day or two. It seems to be becoming more of a viable option."

"What you're feeling is normal," she said, offering me comfort. "I went through the same fight with myself about my job, so I totally get it. Just give it time. It'll work itself out."

I often found myself distracted, thinking about my mom and all the things I wished I could tell her, wondering what I was supposed to be doing, questioning whether or not we could take care of Nana adequately in the cottage, and somewhat habitually, I thought about Miles. I didn't want to, but he seemed to be a constant presence in my head no matter how hard I tried to push him out.

CHAPTER TWO

We'd hit it off immediately, and I didn't even blush when I remembered some of the times I'd offered to have a vacation fling with him. Always the gentleman, he stayed close while keeping his distance. With our crazy compatibility, I never could figure out what kept him from taking me up on my blatant offers, but he did it in such a way as to never make me feel foolish.

Over the past several weeks, my employees had been coming up with great designs, but my head wasn't in it. I was thirty-two and empty inside. Is this what depression looks like? I'd never been disheartened in my life, but I knew I hated this feeling. One afternoon when I should've been concentrating on an upcoming deadline, I picked up my purse and walked out. The blond-brick building I found myself in front of had seemed like the perfect solution a month ago. I went in unannounced. Nana was lifeless, and the nurse leaving the room would only respond to my questions with the standard refrain - they sedate the runners. My decision was made.

"I'm bringing her out, Jordan. I can't let them keep doing this to her."

"We'll get things finished up. When do you think you'll be here?"

"I talked to her doctor. He said she shouldn't fly, but we can drive if I insist on relocating her."

"You're doing the right thing. We'll do everything we can to help. Do you want me to fly out there to drive back with you?"

"Always the faithful friend. No, I want to leave first thing in the morning. But thank you. I love you."

"It's gonna be okay, darlin', I promise."

"I feel good about this decision. Plan on seeing us in about four days."

"You got it. We'll have everything ready. And if you need anything at all, just let me know."

The skilled team who worked for me met to discuss the pros and cons of my missing yet another meeting, but it couldn't be helped. I let Crandon's, our biggest national client, know their account would continue to be handled in a competent manner while I dealt with an emergency that would have me away for the next few weeks.

Packed and ready for an adventure, I arrived unexpectedly at the nursing home early the next morning in a rented van with a bed set up in the back. Nana was unresponsive and unmoving. If I hadn't seen her pulse beating in her neck, I would have believed she was dead. The doctor arrived and confirmed she could be released to my care, and I felt like a freed prisoner as we set out on our adventure.

The first two days were difficult but uneventful. Nana slept most of the trip as time and miles flew by. On the third day, close enough to feel the excitement of arriving at the next chapter of our lives, the medications had worked their way through her system. Trying to keep her calm, reminding her often of who I was, I tried to make a game out of escaping to a new and exciting destination, but the third day was a challenge of monumental proportions.

When she finally fell asleep again, I called Jordan to let her know we would be there soon. She was delighted, and even through the fatigue and stress of the past few days, I was looking forward to being around friends, getting Nana settled in a venue where she wouldn't always be in a stupor, relaxing, and planning our new reality.

The majestic Queen Anne Victorian Jordan had inherited from a long-lost aunt was even more beautiful than the last time I'd seen it, and pulling into the parking lot of Madeline Manor felt like coming home. It was painted in soothing yellows with graduated tones of green highlights. The sparkling windows reflected the sun, and its warm welcome was mystical.

Jordan ran to meet me, and we hugged and cried as though it had been years. My heart stopped, then raced, as my eyes caught those of Miles standing on the steps, his endearing smile conveying comfort and understanding. When he opened his arms, I walked, trancelike, into his waiting embrace. Our previous meetings had been electric, but he was also every security imaginable.

As he squeezed my tired body, the car door closed. We all turned in the direction of the tiny lady standing in her bathrobe with the regalness of a queen. "Hello,

Miles. Do you remember me? We met at Thanksgiving. I'm Elizabeth," Nana said, extending her hand.

"Well, blow me over with a feather," I said under my breath.

"Of course I remember you, dear lady," Miles said, taking her hand and kissing her on the cheek. "We've been preparing for you for days."

"Hello, Brandan," she said to Jordan's husband as he came down the stairs. "So good to see you." We were all stunned to silence at how lucid she was as she hugged Jordan and said, "It's been way too long, my dear. You've never looked better. Married life obviously agrees with you."

"Oh, Nana, it's so good to see you!" Jordan said, squeezing her for all she was worth.

A middle-aged woman followed down the steps and introduced herself as Miriam, the nurse who'd be taking care of Nana. Before my eyes I could see the woman I'd known all my life disappear again behind a mask of mental deterioration. Tears choked me as Nana said, "Janet will be back in a few minutes, she's gone to pick up Jeni from school."

With compassion and understanding, Miles diverted me. "Let's get your things unpacked and into the cottage. We've all been working to make it homey for

Elizabeth and Miriam. We've got you set up in the big house. Thought it would give them an opportunity to get to know each other while you're still here."

The overgrown, abandoned cottage I remembered from my last visit had become an inviting retreat of tranquil beauty. The large, sunny living room was a tasteful combination of vintage and new, and the exquisite antique, navy and teal fireplace was inviting with its flickering flames. "Brandan and I ran a gas line so no one needs to haul wood," Miles said. "Fires are often restful, and this way she can enjoy one whenever she wants."

"Thank you," I said, squeezing his hand. "Let's get her clothes unpacked so we can get her cleaned up. It's been a long three days."

"I can't imagine what it's been like," he said sympathetically. "I'm so proud of you, not only for getting her here, but for making the decision in the first place."

Tears again threatened at his tender concern. Trying to shake off the mood, I laughed and said, "I wished many times that someone had been taking a video of our trip. It would've made a blockbuster movie."

Jordan and Brandan came in carrying the last of the luggage, and Miriam was leading Nana. "Oh, Janet," Nana said to Miriam as she walked through the door, "thank you for bringing me home. It's just the way I remember it." More than anything had in a while, her words brought peace to my heart.

The cottage was an Arts and Crafts bungalow set some distance behind the main house. At the back of the house were two bedrooms with a bath between them, a large claw-foot tub setting a cozy welcome. The kitchen and dining area separated the living room from the sleeping quarters. Much larger than it appeared from the outside, the living room had a wall of windows on the left to let in an abundance of sunlight to reflect on the impressive, Van Briggle tiled fireplace on the opposite wall. Someone had built a wrap-around porch since the last time I'd been here. The cottage was tasteful and tranquil.

Nana caught a glimpse of herself in the mirror. "How wonderful!" she exclaimed. "Henry's still here."

"Where is he, Nana?" I asked quietly.

"He's right there, of course," she said, pointing to her reflection in the mirror.

"Why don't you take your things to the main house while Elizabeth and I get settled," Miriam said kindly. I liked her, and Nana seemed to as well.

"Was Henry your grandfather?" Miles asked as the four of us walked the distance to Madeline Manor.

"Yeah, he died when I was a little girl. I remember him fondly, but I especially remember how devoted they were to each other."

"She seemed comfortable, and it's good you'll be staying in the main house so there aren't even more changes for her when you leave," Jordan said.

"How long you staying?" Miles asked, twirling my long, light brown hair around his fingers.

"A week or two, not sure yet. And what are you doing, looking at how dirty my hair is?"

"Not at all," he laughed. "I was so used to seeing it up, I'm just surprised at how long it is, that's all."

"If I didn't feel like the dregs at the bottom of the pot, I'd say something ingenious. As it is, I'm happy just to be putting one foot in front of the other."

"I put her in The Big Apple," Jordan called to Brandan as he carried my bags through the kitchen.

"Oh, Jordan, I forgot how stunning it is in here." The granite glistened and sunlight reflected off imbedded specks of mica, appliances were state-of-the-art, and polished cherry cabinets reflected a warm patina. "There's so much life in here. The guys did an amazing job."

"Yeah, I like to think it was all my idea, but they knew what they were doing, and there's not a day goes by it doesn't astonish me all over again."

Miles was staring at me, and my heart hammered just the same as it had the first time I laid eyes on him in this very kitchen. "You still have the ability to take my breath away, mister. Better look away or I may have to take you up on the offer that's in your eyes."

"Not an offer, just appreciating what I'm seeing," he said with a sexy, lopsided smile that did strange things to my chest.

"Well, good. You'd be wise not to sleep with me because you'd fall in love, I'd be gone, and where would that leave you?"

Everyone laughed as Brandan came back into the room. "Ah, Jeni, we've missed your wit. Glad to see you and Miles are still shooting sparks."

"It's hard to even say things like that with a straight face after that gruesome trip. Give me time to rest and get cleaned up, change out of the clothes I've been wearing for three days, and I'll see if I can't sharpen my claws on your friend there."

Joey, Jordan's assistant Innkeeper, came in from his basement apartment. "Hey, good to see you!" he said, giving me a hug. "Jordan told me why you're here, and I want you to know we'll all take great care of her."

"Thank you." I held on to him, grateful for the support. "Oh, and you're welcome. I understand you get some time off because I'm visiting."

"You rock. Yep, going on a road trip to Flagstaff. Leaving tomorrow."

"Dinner's ready," Jordan said. "Go get washed up and we'll relax and you can tell us all about your harrowing journey."

As Miles and I headed out of the kitchen, he said, "We set up an intercom system so Miriam can contact the house if she ever needs anything. We also have a backup nurse who'll come by tomorrow and get to know Nana while you're still here."

"I wish it was just your pretty face that intrigued me," I said, staring into his cognac-colored eyes. "You're deliciously thoughtful. I can't thank you enough for your help."

"It's my pleasure," he said in a voice made for whispering naughty things. He wrapped me in his arms. "I'm sorry about your mom, Jeni. I had time to prepare last year before I lost mine, but I can't imagine the shock of what you went through. I'm here if you ever want to talk."

I started bawling like a baby. The floodgates opened, and I was afraid I wasn't going to be able to close them. The past three days had not only been stressful, but I was tired to the bone and hadn't let myself cry deeply since she died. Miles' understanding embrace released it.

"It's okay," he said softly, rocking me. He held my head against his shoulder until his shirt was wet with tears, then led me to the room where I'd be staying, handed me tissues, and turned on the cold water. "After dinner you can soak in the big tub if you want, but right now some cold water might refresh you. I'll meet you in the dining room."

Ten minutes later I was in a change of clothes and we were sitting around the antique mahogany table Jordan had found as the perfect complement to the fretwork in the doorways and the Victorian fireplace. Laughing through dinner with flickering candlelight and a fire in the fireplace felt lighthearted, a sentiment long forgotten.

"So tell me, Brandan. How are you feeling? You appear to be fully recovered from your accident."

"Yeah, I turned a corner last month," he said. "I'm able to walk without a cane, and I'm back to work full time the past few weeks. Jordan runs a tight ship, so I don't get too far out of line." He ran a finger sweetly down her nose. My heart constricted at how much they loved each other, and I looked away, not wanting to intrude on their moment.

"We've all been reading about the symptoms of dementia and how best to react to her," Jordan said, breaking eye contact with her husband.

Tears threatened again. "No words in my vocabulary can adequately express my gratitude for everything you guys have done."

"You've got a lot on your plate right now, and the cottage seems a suitable solution."

"One of the things Miles has been talking to Miriam about," said Jordan, "is available medications, and the pros and cons of each."

Yawning, I said, "I can't wait for you to share your insight."

"Plenty of time for that," Miles said, helping me to my feet. "Let's get you to bed and I'll come back tomorrow."

"I appreciate your offer," I said with a tired smile, "but I *do* need to help Jordan clean up."

"Don't even think about it," she said as she and Brandan carried plates to the kitchen. "I'm giving Joey a few weeks off while you're here so I'm going to let him clean up tonight. I'll put you to work after you've had a good night's sleep." She blew me a kiss.

CHAPTER THREE

"I'm not sure when the last time was I slept like that," I said. "Only the delectable smells wafting from your kitchen penetrated my consciousness. Can I help?"

"So glad you slept! I have all the ingredients out if you want to throw together some of your famous muffins. Have to admit I've been looking forward to you showing me a few of your tricks."

"Twist my arm. The thought of having a kitchen like this and time to cook makes my heart do a happy dance. Thanks!"

"And you can have the room for however long you want. March is a slow month, so we don't have many guests on the books yet."

"Okay, tell me the truth. How do you like being here?"

"Oh, Jeni," she said, a wistful look reflecting what was obviously in her heart. "Everything we experience in our lives goes into making us who we become, but I'm where I belong. A successful career was my goal, but now I've found my dream. I love what I'm doing, I love being a wife. Someday I may dabble at being a lawyer again, but I'm content in all ways."

"You don't feel like you're missing something? Like you live in the back of beyond?"

"Good grief, no! I'm not sure there's an area of my life that isn't perfectly satisfied. I love the town, the people in it, the B and B, being Brandan's wife."

Her words set off tiny feelings of discontent, or maybe it was a slight case of envy because she'd started on her future, and I couldn't even bring shadows of mine into focus. "I couldn't be more pleased for you, genuinely," I said, the scent of coffee teasing my nostrils.

"And I couldn't have walked in at a better time," Brandan said, kissing his wife long enough for me to appreciate his sincere devotion to her. "You might say we were thunderstruck and never recovered." They laughed at whatever their private joke was, and my heart constricted because there was no white-picket fence in my future. I had chosen a different path, and it didn't include a forever relationship.

The backdoor opened to cheerful banter between Miles and Nana. The early red sunlight crept across the cloudy sky. "I thought I'd bring her over for breakfast and give Miriam a break."

"You'd be in big trouble if I was sticking around," I said quietly. "Thank you."

"You're welcome. Besides, Elizabeth and I are old friends, isn't that right, Elizabeth?"

Everyone laughed, but the look on her face was one of bewilderment. "Of course, Henry, it's been almost sixty years now."

"Nana, that's Miles."

The shake of his head was slight, and I let it go in the joy of the moment. This was a treasure of people and I was so thankful I'd decided to bring her here. "Do you know there's a man in the clock?" Nana said matter-of-factly as we finished eating.

"Really?" I asked. "What does he look like?"

"Well, Henry, of course. When I wound the clock, he invited me to come in with him, but I told him there was no way we could both fit."

We ended up eating in the dining room, and the time was filled with merriment and sharing favorite memories.

"Jeni and I were called 'The JJ's' in college," Jordan said.

"But we thought of ourselves as 'M and M's,'" I interjected, "for 'Mischief Makers.'"

"Professors gave us wide berth when they saw us in the hallways together," Jordan continued, laughing at the memory, "knowing disruption wouldn't be far behind."

"Oh! Did you ever hear the story of the 'Unvites'?" I asked Miles.

"No, but I can't wait." His smile reached his golden eyes as our eyes met.

"Neither can I," I said under my breath. Everyone laughed as Brandan encouraged me to leave the poor boy alone and get on with the story.

"Yeah, he looks totally defenseless to me," I said. "Anyway, Jordan was engaged before she met Brandan - a hoity toity New York lawyer who worked for her dad. Three weeks before the wedding she saw him kissing another woman."

"So Jeni designed these 'Unvites'," Jordan took over the story, "to send to the invited guests. I would have paid a substantial amount of money to have been a fly on the wall when the gentleman in question, and I use the term lightly, found out he was now the EX-fiancé as he opened his Unvite and saw a picture of himself kissing someone else."

"You mean that's how he found out?" Miles asked, astonished. "That would have been worth the price of admission. Good job!" He winked at me. My heart did a spiral dance. "By the way, Jordan, these are the best muffins I've ever put in my mouth. What are they?"

"Jeni made them."

"They're Banana Blueberry Pecan," I said.

"I may have to stop by every morning if this is what it's gonna be like."

"Yeah, that'd be a hardship."

Amid the laughter, I said in a slightly more serious tone. "I'm sorry I've been teasing you so unmercifully. You're so nice about it, but I'll stop if it bothers you."

"When it bothers me, I'll let you know. Deal?"

"Deal."

After Miriam came to walk Nana back to the cottage, Miles and I had a few minutes alone. "You can certainly handle Nana however you want, but I think it's easier not to argue with her when she tells you things. Call it little white lies, if you will, but she's muddled enough, and trying to explain how she's wrong will only intensify the confusion."

"That makes perfect sense. Mom was so good at letting her talk. I'd be frustrated the fifth time Nana would ask what day of the week it was, but mom's solution was to write it down for her. She never seemed to get frustrated and she never lost her temper."

Brandan and Jordan came back to help clear the table, and Miles continued. "Sounds like your mom understood. It must be frustrating for Nana, and it would only agitate her more if you were short tempered and she had no idea what she'd done. Staying calm helps set the tone. And you know she's not doing it on purpose. I've learned some pointers I'll be happy to share."

"You're always welcome to share your pointer with me." Even I laughed at how brazen I was being with him. "Sorry, Miles. You know I'm kidding – sort of." Miles was shaking his head as he and Brandan got ready to leave.

"Miles and I are working in Niwot today," Brandan said, kissing Jordan's cheek, "so I shouldn't be too late. Jack and Callie would like to come over one night this week to see Jeni, so pick a day and I'll let them know."

"That will be wonderful," I said as I continued to clear the table. "You're invited, too."

"Thanks," Miles said. "I'll be around as much as I can." With a smirk he said, "I'm rather fond of your grandmother." He laughed as I threw a napkin at his retreating back.

"Glad to see the crazy attraction is still there between you," Jordan said when we were alone in the kitchen as I set dishes on the glistening countertop. "I'm not sure why, but Brandan says Miles isn't looking for even a temporary relationship, but when the sparks fly between you, I'm not sure how he can possibly resist."

"As much as he does outrageous things to my head and my body, and as nice as he is, I can't imagine getting involved with anyone right now, Jord. I go to bed tired, I wake up tired, and the eighteen hours in between are cram packed."

"Let's at least break *that* cycle while you're here. Let's send you back relaxed and ready to take on the world again as only my Jeni knows how."

"Then maybe some mindless sex with Miles is *exactly* what I need," I teased.

"Somehow he doesn't strike me as a casual sex kinda guy, and you might burn the house down it's so hot between you."

"He sure flips my switches, that's for sure."

"You were like magnet and steel when you met. Brandan and I laughed about it for days."

"Yeah, there's something about him. It's not even because he's handsome, there's just this overall attraction that's consuming."

"I feel that way about Brand. Still do after all this time."

"I'd be lying if I weren't looking forward to appreciating the eye candy. And he's so flippin' nice. I've *never* been attracted to nice guys. What's that about?"

"Maybe you're growing up. Maybe you're learning things about yourself. But any way you look at it, you couldn't go wrong with Miles. He really is a great guy."

"Yeah, in my dreams. Life in New York is a full-time job. No time for a relationship or even to daydream about one."

"I've got everything cleaned up and put away, but I can't find the salt shaker. Any idea where it is?" Jordan asked as she hung the towel on the rack.

"No. Only the pepper shaker was on the table when I cleared it. You sure it was there?"

"Yeah, they were both there, but no worries, it'll turn up."

"Do you mind if I take a nap? Can't figure out why I'm so tired."

"Oh, I imagine that's common after three long days in a van driving across country with a patient in the back. To say nothing of the altitude. I've got some stuff to take care of, your job is to relax."

Several hours later I was feeling fantastic. I made calls to my office, answered emails, drew an ad campaign I'd been tossing around in my head, then decided to wander. The walk to town was less than a mile, and one of the comforts I remembered from my last visit was Sam at the Amber Rose. I stood back to hold the door open for a girl in a bikini top, short shorts, and cowboy boots that came to her knees. I couldn't help but think of the Naked Cowboy who strummed his guitar in Times Square for money. The association made me laugh.

"Well, well, if it ain't Miss Jeni come for a visit. How you doing, young lady?" he asked, coming around the counter and giving me a hug. "Callie said you'd be bringing your grandma. How was the trip?"

"Not an experience I'd ever want to repeat, but you know what they say, what doesn't kill you makes you stronger."

"That much fun, huh? Heard you got yourself a good nurse."

Looking around at the sunlit wood benches and the highly polished countertops, I remembered how much I enjoyed its coziness. "Yeah, I'm thrilled with Miriam. The guys have set up safeguards in case Nana escapes. She has a problem with not staying where she's supposed to be. I wanted you to be on alert in case you ever see her down here alone, it's because she's on the loose."

"We'll let everybody know. You know how it is 'round here – it's all family. Everyone'll keep an eye out. How long you stayin'?"

"Maybe ten days, two weeks. I'll play it by ear."

"It's a big responsibility what you got left with," he said, pouring me a cup of his famous coffee. It'd be hard on anybody, but you ownin' a company in New York, your ma dyin' like that, you sure got my sympathy. Can't be easy."

I fought tears. "Thanks, Sam. Please don't be too sympathetic. It seems to make me cry. We all have our issues. I think they call it 'life,' huh?"

In his lovable way he said, "You let me know anything you might need. Me an' Sunni can fill in if you ever need us."

"Thank you. I appreciate that. I'll bring Nana down to see you soon. Maybe if we can make things more familiar it will help settle her."

"Ain't gonna be easy, but we'll do what we can. You come back any time."

There were less than fifteen hundred people who inhabited the enclave of Nederland, and everyone I'd met had been unfailingly kind and friendly. I was heading back to the cottage when the phone rang with an unfamiliar number. "Hey, Jeni, it's Miles."

The sound of his voice made me feel like I'd been running. "Well, that's interesting. You don't even have to be standing here to make my breath catch," I said.

There was a short pause. "I see you left your filter in New York."

"Nah, I gave mine back. Life's a lot more fun when you say what you're thinking. At least as long as it's not hurting anyone. I'm not hurting you, am I?"

"No, I'm a big boy. I think I can handle whatever your tongue can dish out."

"Well, well. Big boy and tongue in the same sentence. I like where this conversation is headed."

"Stop it, brat. I'm calling to see if you want me to take you to return the rental. I've got some time and thought you might like a ride into Boulder to take it back."

"Good grief, Miles. How the hell are you still running loose? Why hasn't someone snatched you up by now? What's the matter with the women around here?"

When he didn't respond, I said, "Wait, you're not married, are you?"

"No, I'm not married. I'll see you in an hour."

There was someone else in the cottage when Miriam answered the door. "Hey, Jeni. Come in. I'd like you to meet Francine. She's going to be helping with Elizabeth's care." I liked her on sight, and as we shook hands, Nana came out of the kitchen.

"Anyone seen the cat?"

Miriam and Francine looked at each other and Miriam said, "We let the cat out a while ago. It should be back soon."

"Okay," Nana said as she headed toward the back of the house.

"That was brilliant. I'm still of a mindset that my first response would've been to tell her we don't have a cat."

"Doesn't do any good to cause more confusion," said Francine. "Let go of your preconceived notions of truth and time because they have their own. Takes care of a lot of frustration for everyone."

"What a relief to know she'll be in such capable hands when I'm gone. I'll visit as often as possible, but in the meantime, it's a gift to know you and Miriam are here with her."

"You can't change anything that's going on here or in her head. Feel good about the care you're providing her. You stepped up to the plate and made a good decision. You're not in a position to walk away from your life for who-knows-how-long to nurse her. Let us do our job, you do yours."

"Thank you. I know you're right. I keep thinking of the professional care I had for her before, and it horrifies me."

"She's in good hands now. We'll keep her as calm as possible. We try hard not to correct or agitate, just to understand where she is in her world at any given point in time."

"I obviously have a lot to learn."

"We've dealt with it for years. Don't beat yourself up."

"Come over in the morning for breakfast, if you'd like," I said. "Jordan has the market cornered on delicious."

"We'll try to get Elizabeth out as often as possible, and routine is good for her. I'll work at least two days each week, more if needed," said Francine. "Miriam and I have worked together before, so don't worry, we have this covered."

"There aren't enough words," I said.

The wind filled the trees with a rustling murmur and lifted my hair in wisps out of the pencil I used to hold it up. The surroundings were lush green as I walked the long trek back to Madeline Manor. Leaves were beginning to bud on the aspen, but there were still deep layers on the ground to crunch under my feet. Jordan and Brandan had ten acres, and the cottage was set well back from the main house, the backdrop idyllic.

The sun reflected off the water in the distance like chilled steel. Diamonds appeared to shimmer on the gentle ripples. I was lost in its promise as Miles pulled into the drive.

CHAPTER FOUR

A broad smile lit my face when he got out of his car. "Ready?"

"When you're around, always," I teased. "Let me get my keys and the address."

When I came out, Miles was talking to the young neighbor boy, James Gabriel. "Hey, Jeni. My mom said I could come up and talk to Nana. You know where she is?"

"Well, hi! It's good to see you, and that's very nice of you. She's in the cottage."

"Me and Nana go way back. See ya later," he said, running off.

"I guess you never know whose life you touch," he said. "That's pretty special."

"Yeah, I'll be thinking of that one for a while. I hope she remembers something about him, but even when she was muddled with him before, he seemed to roll with the punches."

I handed Miles the address. "I know exactly where this is," he said. "Want to follow me?"

"Sure, thanks. They're open for a while, so I appreciate you thinking of it. And Jordan said I could use her cherry red truck if I need wheels. An offer like that makes this monstrosity a has-been. Besides which, the sooner the horror of those three days driving across country in this van is gone from the forefront of my mind, the better." I followed him through the winding roads of Boulder Canyon, spectacular at any time, but even more so with the golden rays of the setting sun playing hide-and-seek over mountains and through trees.

After we'd finished the paperwork and were heading back to Nederland, I asked, "Do you ever get tired of the magnificence of your surroundings?"

"I've been here most of my life, and every time I drive the Canyon I see something new."

"It's so different than what I know." Was that wistfulness in my voice?

"This must seem like such an altered state to you. I've been to New York a few times, and for me it's the classic, 'It's a nice place to visit, but . . .'"

"I guess it's what you're used to. Tell me about yourself. We've got this wild connection and I'd sleep with you in a heartbeat, but I don't really know anything about your life. Spill the beans."

The deep, rich timber of his laugh made my heart happy.

"Not much to tell. Brandan and I've worked for Jack for a decade now. Brandan's the foreman for the Denver area, I oversee the construction projects for everywhere else. Sometimes we work together, sometimes we go weeks without seeing each other."

"And you're not married?"

"You've asked me before, and the answer's still no," he said. "How about you?"

"Nah, never have been. Never met anyone worth sticking around for. I tend to pick the jerks, the narcissists who think they're the center of the known universe, the ones who are emotionally unavailable. Like the last one, Jared, who couldn't figure out why it upset me that he slept with someone else. And the double whammy was the 'someone else' was a colleague I thought I was close to."

"Ouch," he said. "I'm sorry that happened to you. Sometimes the cruelty of mankind amazes me."

"Isn't that the truth?"

Taking the hairpin turns in the dark like a pro, he asked, "What do you want from life? I know it's been a rough time lately, but are you doing what you want?"

"As long as I've been aware, I've wanted to use my creativity. Not necessarily all day every day like I have been, but you get the drift. I joined a friend and we started an ad agency. It took off, then so did she. The days after she left were dark. She wore down in a hurry, so I bought her out."

"How long ago was that?"

"It's been about five years. I now have ten great employees, and most hours of most days are spent being 'on' – 'on' for clients, 'on' coming up with ad campaigns, 'on' for people who need me. May be true for most jobs, but this time of being 'off' has been a blessing – even though I've been doing work from here, it's not nearly as stressful."

"I'm not being flip when I say that using your brain is as exhausting, if not more so, than hard physical labor," he said sympathetically. "I don't mind people, but if I had to think and interact and please that much, I'd probably go into shutdown mode."

"Tell me about it. Some days I want to lock the door and tell them to leave me alone. Since my mom died and I've had Nana to worry about, it's even more concentrated."

"You know she'll be in good hands. There are already so many here who care for her – including James Gabriel. How cute was that?"

There were those damn tears again. "There's so much conflict in me. Leaving her for someone else to care for, going seventeen hundred miles across country so I'm not readily available, knowing I have to get back, having to sort through my mom's house and figure out what to do with everything, launching this ad campaign we worked so hard to get."

"The sorting was the worst part for me," he said. "My situation was different, but it's never easy losing a parent. We knew for a long time she had cancer, and the last few months she was pretty weak."

"Did you have anyone to help?"

"One sister, but she had her own issues at the time being bedridden with a pregnancy. Jack was great about giving me as much time off as I needed, and Brandan filled in a lot of the gaps. I had the joy and the heartache of going through her possessions with her. She'd tell me who to give things to or what to donate. You've got a whole different scenario in front of you. Do *you* have anyone to help?"

"No. I've got a lot of friends, but Jordan's the only one I'd want with me, so I'll take a few days when I get back and try not to think too hard about what I'm doing."

He was so kind. "There will be healing in being aware of what you're doing. Remember her and what you shared as you go through her things. Remember how much she loved you, the good times. Store those treasured memories away somewhere so you can take them off your mental shelf every now and then."

"I knew I was attracted to you, but you're delightfully sensible too."

"Is that what makes you so good as an ad exec – your lack of a verbal filter?" he asked, laughing.

"I do tend to say things that lead to other thoughts, and that's where a lot of my creativity comes from. I used to try to filter, but life's not as much fun that way. Does it bother you?"

"Not in the least. It's a huge part of your charm."

"Are you for real? Can I keep you?"

His rumbling laugh did strange things to my insides. His chiseled face came in and out of the shadows from the passing headlights, and when he caught his lower lip between his teeth, my breathing stopped.

"Sure you don't want to sleep together before I go back?"

We were coming in to Nederland, and he pulled over to the parking lot that bordered Barker Reservoir. A slight breeze disturbed the water, and a carnival of lights twinkled as if by magic on the surface. He put the car in park and faced me.

"I'm going to try this unfiltered routine for a minute," he said, tenderly touching my face. "I've never met anyone like you, you know that. We're both aware the world started spinning a little faster when we met. There's nothing I'd like better than to take you up on what you're offering, but it's not gonna happen."

I came back to earth with a small crash as regret blinded me momentarily. "Listen to me," he said. "It's obvious I like you – a lot. You make me feel things I didn't know existed. But I'm not looking for quick sex, and you're leaving. I don't do casual relationships, and I have no intention of starting now."

"I'd make sure the sex wasn't quick," I teased, wondering what there was about him that made me want to push the envelope.

"No, I imagine we'd give a new definition to an all-nighter," he said warmly. "But let's leave it at knowing there's this intense thing, and enjoy the rest of it."

"I'll have to wrap my brain around that for a while."

"I suppose it wouldn't help you to know I'm in love with your mind and I want to make love to your thoughts?" he teased.

Coloring with pleasure, our gazes locked in mutual desire. "Will you at least kiss me?" I asked, lips parting expectantly.

"That would be an incredibly stupid thing to do." His eyes hooded as he leaned closer, his thumb still stroking my cheek. "Sometimes I think there must be magnets in our lips because I want to kiss you every time I'm with you."

"You'll get no argument from me."

"Not if you have half the pull I feel." His eyes opened momentarily, their caress as tangible as the trace of his hand. "I'm not feeling too smart right this minute," he whispered, close enough to feel his breath.

Part of me wanted to delay the kiss I'd wanted for so long. The glorious sensation of anticipation had my cells humming, and my imagination was going wild as I stared at his tongue that crossed first his lower lip, then upper. My faint whimper must've triggered his impatience as he yielded to the inevitable. His lips covered mine, hot, soft, devouring, passionate.

In my dreams I couldn't have anticipated how my body would react to the simple touch of his lips. I wanted him with a whole new level of desire. What was it about this gentle man that produced such a violent reaction in me?

As I moved into the kiss, wanting more, pressing harder, his hands cupped my face as his kiss gentled. "We knew it would be like this," he said through labored breathing, resting his forehead against mine.

"You can't be serious - you're going to stop?" Yes, I heard the pleading in my voice.

"Jeni . . . Jeni. We need to get back. Let's not make it any harder than it already is . . . so to speak," he said, smiling tenderly.

I was taking deep breaths, trying to gain control of my raging pulse as he put the car in gear and drove the last mile or so into town. Turning up the road that led to Madeline Manor, he said, "It's never boring with you, is it?"

"It could be so much more exciting, though. On more than one occasion, Jordan has said we're like magnet and steel."

Our attention was distracted by a small crowd standing in the parking lot of the Inn. Fearful something had happened to Nana, I hurried to Jordan's side.

"Hey, Jeni. Everything's okay. Miriam used the bathroom and when she came out Nana was gone. She called and searched frantically, then used the intercom to put us on alert. I came into the kitchen, and there she was, sitting at the table in her nightgown. Said she'd come over with Henry."

Miles heard part of the conversation. "Do you think we need to put a deadbolt on the doors to the cottage?" he asked. "Not something I want to do, but we may have to. Hate the thought of it, but we can't have her wandering around in the woods."

"Miles and I will figure out the best way to make it safe," Brandan said. "Safe from her escaping, and safe so they're able to get out if there's a need."

"Thank you. What would I do without you guys?" I asked, overwhelmed with love for these people.

"It'll shock you how creative they get when they want to go somewhere," Miles said. "Miriam will need relief often. It'll be a full-time job making sure Nana doesn't stray."

"While I'm still here, I'll take her for walks. Not sure whether that will satisfy or activate her need-to-wander switch, but she's still agile. It'll be fun and it'll give Miriam free time."

Everyone had an opinion about that, and it was a while before we headed into the house. "Will you stay for a while?" I asked as Miles turned to leave.

"No, I'm late getting back. I'll drop in tomorrow."

"Hey!" He turned with a smile and a questioning raise of a brow.

"Thank you," I said sincerely. We held each other's gaze. I had the feeling he wanted to stay as much as I wanted him to.

"See you tomorrow."

Jordan was standing in the kitchen when I walked in. "You've got it bad, girl," she said with a sympathetic look.

"I might have, but it doesn't matter. I'm leaving soon and he's not looking for a fling."

"Brandan's never shared Miles' story with me, but he insists Miles is quite comfortable being single and unencumbered."

"That's pretty much what Miles told me this evening. Ce la vie. Like I need another complication in my life right now."

"Talk about a complication – you wouldn't know what to do with someone as nice as Miles, would you? Can't imagine how that would work out for you," she said affectionately.

She was prepping food for breakfast. We spent a while talking about some of the fiasco dates I'd been on. The whole time we talked, Brandan found a way to touch her whenever he was near.

"Could you have imagined a year ago you'd be so happy in this Victorian mansion in the middle of nowhere, fixing breakfast for guests?" I asked.

"Never. I had my life planned out in boardrooms and courtrooms, not breakfast and caretaking. Wouldn't change it for the world."

"I couldn't be happier for you," I said. I kissed them both on the cheek and headed off for bed.

CHAPTER FIVE

After a leisurely breakfast of ginger pancakes with homemade blueberry maple syrup, I wanted to spend time with Nana. "Would you like to walk to town? It's a beautiful day and we don't have to be gone long."

"That would be lovely, let me get my sweater," she said.

We took our time meandering and ended up at the water's edge. "Do you remember when you were six, and we were on vacation at Lake Chotard in Vicksburg, Mississippi? We were standing on the water's edge just like this when you swung around with your fishing pole and caught your hook in my arm. I still have the scar," she said, rubbing her upper right arm.

My heart did a dash as she reminded me of that youthful memory, one I had long forgotten. These glimpses of the woman I knew were precious and fleeting. "Oh, Nana, of course I do. I was so heart-

broken to have hurt you, and I remember how sweet
you were to me as mama cut the barb off so she could
back the hook out. I was much more upset than you
seemed to be."

She took my hand as we headed toward town. I
wanted to hold on to this woman and not let go. "Do
you remember you bought me ice cream that
afternoon," I asked, "and sang to me and rocked me to
sleep because I was so upset?"

"What afternoon, dear?"

"The afternoon at Lake Chotard."

"Where?" She was gone again, but I would hold onto
this precious window I'd had into the woman she once
was.

As we got close to the Amber Rose, Sam was
backing out of the parking lot. "Hop in," he said, out of
breath. "Y'all need to get back to the Manor."

"What happened?" I asked anxiously, knowing
something had to be terribly wrong for the calm and
laid-back proprietor to be hurrying to help Nana into
the passenger seat of his Jeep. "Jordan's been trying to
call you. I told her I'd find you and bring you home."
He made sure I was sitting down before he floored it
and took off at speeds that exceeded my comfort level
on the back roads.

"I turned my phone off. Has something happened to Brandan? What is it, Sam?"

"I'll let her tell you, but Brandan's fine," he said, screeching to a halt as we arrived. "You get yourself on in there. I'll take Elizabeth . . . go," he said as he helped me out of the back seat.

Running through the house, I called out to find where she was. "We're up in Willow's Nest." I recognized Callie's voice as I hurried to Jordan's third-floor bedroom.

The room was in chaos with clothes everywhere and two suitcases open on the bed. "What's going on, Jord?" I asked, giving Callie a hug. It was a shame to meet her again under such chaotic conditions, but it was obvious Jordan had been crying, so I turned to Brandan questioningly.

"It's Riley," he said quietly.

"Daddy's had a heart attack," Jordan said. "Mom says it's touch and go. I'm so sorry, but I have to leave," she said, crying again.

"Don't be silly! Of course you have to go! Tell me what needs to be done and I'll do it."

She threw her arms around me and sobbed. "Oh, honey, I tried to call you but it kept going to voicemail. Brandan and I got a flight out of Denver this afternoon. Joey won't be back for at least a week, so Callie's going to fix breakfast for the guests, and I'll make arrangements to have someone come in and clean between shifts."

"You won't do any such thing. I happen to be an excellent cook and pretty meticulous, so you catch your plane and I'll take care of everything here."

"I couldn't possibly ask you to do that."

"You didn't ask and I'm taking over, so don't argue. I have at least a week left here, and if it's longer than that, we'll figure something else out. Now what can I do to help?" I asked in the midst of the whirlwind of activity.

"Nothing really. I think Brandan and I are almost done."

"Then Callie and I will get out of your way. Let me know if you need anything at all."

The sweet sounds of a baby could be heard as I came down the stairs. "Is that Charlotte Rose?" I asked Callie.

"It sure is. I set up the crib in The Gables. Come see how big she's gotten."

She was standing in the crib when we walked in. "Mama," she said, lifting her arms in the age-old way babies tell you they want to be picked up. I loved this child. She pulled at my heartstrings, and I went to the crib to oblige. "She's so precious!"

"She's beyond compare," Callie said. "Interested in everything, loves everyone, sleeps eleven hours straight at night, loves routine . . . sometimes I think I'm dreaming, she's such a joy."

When she smiled at me and reached for my hair, my heart melted. "And Jack thinks he invented fatherhood," she went on. "They're so cute together. You wonder how you can contain all the love – for him, for her, for them together – never could've imagined this world existed."

"She's not even mine and I can't define how I feel about her. You're exceedingly blessed."

"Thank you, Jeni," she said, hugging me as she took Charlotte Rose. "I will be here whenever you need me. If you want help cleaning or cooking or doing anything, let me know. And my offer's still open that I'll do this if you don't want to. I understand your plate is full already."

"Thanks, but no. I'm kind of excited about it. I think I'll move my things to The Library on the main floor for convenience, but I have it covered. I promise I'll call if I need you."

When I called Miriam on the intercom, she told me the walk must've worn Nana out, because when Sam brought her in, she sat down in the chair and fell asleep. There were a lot of last-minute instructions as I helped pack the car. Jack had already made arrangements for Brandan's second-in-command to take over while they were gone, so that base was covered.

I loved how, no matter what, these people pulled together. They were as much family as anyone blood-related. I felt privileged to be a part of it, if only for a while. It was a shame the circumstances were difficult, but like everything else, we'd find a way to take care of what needed to be done.

It was not surprising that Jordan was so well organized. Everything was detailed and all I needed to do was implement what she'd already set in motion. There weren't more than a few guests scheduled over the next week, so I wasn't worried it would be stressful. Quite frankly, I was looking forward to the change of pace.

Jordan called to say they'd made it to the airport with plenty of time to spare, and to again let me know how much she appreciated me being there. Standing in the kitchen watching the sun go down a few hours later, I actually enjoyed the racing pulse Miles caused when he came through the back door.

Even with past lovers, no one had affected my whole being like he did. And, dear Lord, he was beautiful. Muscular arms were noticeable under his shirtsleeves. He was tanned with short, dark hair, and eyes the color of honey that changed to molten amber when he looked at me. I really could sit and stare at him for hours.

"How you holding up?" he asked, giving me a hug as he came in the kitchen.

"Keep doing this and I can face anything." I loved standing here with my cheek on his chest, his arms around me.

He tipped my chin up to look at me. "It was kind of you to offer to stay," he said. "I'll help as much as I can."

"It wasn't kind of me. It just is. Jordan and I have had each other's backs for a lot of years. There's never a question of being there for each other no matter the circumstance, we just are. I'm not sure what I would've done with Nana if the cottage hadn't worked out, so don't go thinking I'm a saint. I'm just a good friend." I smiled at him, breath coming a little faster.

"I've always had a philosophy about people who are givers," he said. "Some people think you can give and give and then you run out of giving. But when the giving is with another giver, it's never tit for tat, it just keeps overflowing, replenishing itself. It's pretty remarkable, and that probably made no sense at all."

"It made perfect sense." My arms were wrapped around his waist. "You don't mind if I keep standing here, listening to your voice come from deep in your chest, do you? Besides which, I love the view."

He didn't respond, just held my gaze. "What is it about you that makes me forget my preconceived notions of not getting involved?"

"My personality, charm, and basic enjoyment of uninhibited sex?"

The smile played on his lips before his eyes closed and his lips lowered to mine. "I must've taken leave of my senses," he said, covering my lips with his.

Passion ignited. The moan must've come from my throat, but I was transported. I wanted this man. I pulled his shirttails from his pants and ran my hands up his back. He was warm and firm, my nails scratching as desire erupted. His fingers slid through my hair, bringing my lips closer and harder into his kiss.

"Excuse us, shall we come back?" Miriam said from the doorway.

"We're not gonna leave just because they wanna kiss. They can kiss anytime," Nana said, coming through the back door.

Miriam apologized as Miles turned away to tuck his shirt into his jeans. "Elizabeth wanted to get out of the house and wanted to know if you'd heard anything from Jordan yet." At my look of surprise, she continued. "Your grandmother seems quite fond of Wiley Riley, as she calls him, and wants to make sure he's going to pull through."

"I haven't heard anything yet," I said, feeling disoriented. "I don't expect to hear until later tonight or tomorrow morning."

Nana had gone to the refrigerator and was searching through the contents. "Do you want something to eat, Nana?"

"You got any potato salad left? It's always better the next day. Don't mind if I do," she said, pulling out the container and looking for a plate.

"I need to get going," Miles said.

"Really? Do you have to?" I asked, trying to talk to him with my eyes.

"Sorry, but I do. I'll be around as much as I can to help you run things."

"Come up any time," I said, walking him to the bottom of the steps outside the kitchen. "Day or night, you're always welcome."

"Jeni," he said, then hesitated.

"Yes?"

After a lingering moment, he said, "Nothing, I'll see you tomorrow."

There would be no guests the first two mornings, so I didn't bother setting an alarm. Usually up before dawn, it was almost eight o'clock when I started to regain consciousness. My body obviously knew what it needed to combat shifts in altitude and recent stresses, and I was going to let it take the lead.

The room was comfortable and inviting. Done in deep browns and navy blues, The Library tempted you to pull out one of the hundreds of leather-bound books from the shelf and read. Although I was a fan of reading on my Kindle, there was something alluring about the feel and smell of this vast collection of books that made you want to sit and escape to a world of joined words that wove stories of intrigue or romance.

Centered on the wall between the warm leather overstuffed chairs was a Lincoln Log Quilt made by one of Jordan's ancestors. Brandan had it preserved in a frame, and your eyes could feel the textures and love that wove each stitch. French-doors graced one wall that opened to a wrap-around porch, and a gas fire pit surrounded by wicker chairs was an extension of the invitation to relax and read.

The day ahead had no time commitments except a brief conference call with co-workers, so after a leisurely soak in the over-sized claw-foot tub and a piece of toast and fresh-squeezed orange juice, I strolled along the tree-lined path to the cottage. I could hear voices, so I turned the knob ever so slightly to peek in, trying not to disturb them.

"Do you see him?" Nana was saying to the young James Gabriel. "He's right there," she said, pointing to the small mirror she held.

He leaned closer and looked intently, "I think so, move it just a little bit."

She was moving it around for him. "It's like winding the clock, you have to do it carefully or we'll lose Henry."

A smiling Miriam came out of the kitchen carrying two plates of food and set them on the small table in front of the antique, dark blue and turquoise-tiled Van Briggle fireplace. "Why don't you two come and eat and let's see if we can bring it more into focus?" she said with affection. She saw me standing there. "Good morning, Jeni. Would you like to join us for an early lunch?"

"No, thanks. Everything appears to be under control here. I'm gonna walk to town and have a relaxing day unless you need me for something. I heard from Jordan and they believe Riley is going to pull through. He'll be in the hospital for a few days, but he seems to be out of the woods. It was a close call."

"That's great news!" Miriam said.

"I liked him a lot," James Gabriel said. "I'm glad he's not gonna die. I'd hate for Jordan to lose her dad like I did."

"Your dad would be so proud of how you're growing up. Thanks for spending time with Nana."

"I love being here. Me and Nana share secrets, and she likes havin' me around."

Callie was talking to Sam when I walked into the Amber Rose. Charlotte Rose was on her hip, with Callie's mahogany hair wrapped around her tiny fist, finding its way to her eager mouth. They all turned at the sound of the bell, and the heart-warming welcome touched me to my core. When my eyes watered, Callie, in her forthright manner, said, "What's the matter, darling?"

"I have no idea. I love being here, and the down time's given me a chance to unwind in ways I'd forgotten I could. I seem to cry or tear up all the time, which is strange since I haven't shed a tear in I-don't-remember-how-long."

"Don't beat yourself up, and don't think twice about it. You've been through a lot, and I imagine you haven't had much of a chance to really grieve. Trust me, the littlest things will set you off, and it surprises you that it keeps happening."

"And it was the littlest thing," I laughed. "Seeing Charlotte Rose made me wonder for the first time in a long time what I might be missing. I love kids, and guess I resigned myself to babies being other people's future, not mine. Mind if I hold her?"

"Be my guest."

My heart melted as deep blue eyes locked with mine and a toothless smile spread across her face as she reached for my hair. I nuzzled her nose and she let out a belly laugh, pulling my hair into her mouth.

"She seems comfortable with you," Sam said with his bearded smile. "Kids know who's a friend and who ain't."

"She's a near-perfect human," Callie said lovingly.

"You're obviously doing a great job with her," I said, enthralled. "By the way, I heard from Jordan and it looks like Riley is out of the woods."

"Oh, I'm *so* glad! Any idea when they'll be back?"

"Probably in about a week. I don't have to leave until then, so it'll work out well."

"You gonna eat?" Sam asked.

"No. I'm wandering while I have a chance, but thanks. Miriam seems to be a Godsend, and James Gabriel was sitting at Nana's feet when I left. Leaving will be a lot easier knowing she's in such good hands. Or maybe it's going to be a lot harder," I said.

"I know," Callie said, squeezing my arm. "So glad you made this decision, though. She'll be well-loved here."

"Isn't that the truth? If it can't be me taking care of her, I think I found the best. I wanted to stop in and say 'hi,'" I said, handing Charlotte Rose back to Callie.

"Stop in any time," Sam said. "It's always good to see you."

Callie stopped me as I was leaving. "There are times in our lives when we have big decisions we need to face. Seems like this may be one of those times in your life. I promise it'll work out well," she said with affection.

"Thanks for the encouragement. I know you're right."

CHAPTER SIX

The wind tasted my skin in gentle nips as I walked the short distance to Barker Reservoir. It was a perfect day with a soft breeze stirring the surface of the water, the color reminding me of the fireplace in the cottage. I walked along the shoreline, shoes in hand, feet wet, with thoughts surging through me as though the floodgates had been opened.

Looking over the expanse, I couldn't help but think of Gabe, James Gabriel's dad, who lost his life when this water had been ice and teenagers had fallen through. Gabe was driving by when the ice broke, and was able to get the boys out, but couldn't pull himself out as hypothermia set in. Brandan was able to get him out of the frigid water, but Gabe died on the way to the hospital, leaving behind a pregnant wife and young son. Life seemed so unfair at times.

The lapping water brought a new idea with each push. I thought of the fragility of the mind, and how

my once-brilliant grandmother was now mentally frail.
I wondered how I'd wasted so much of my life on
narcissistic men like 'Jared the Jerk,' as Jordan was
fond of calling him. I'd been avoiding thoughts of time-
sensitive, intense commitments I would have to face
when I got back to New York.

One of those commitments would be sorting through
mom's possessions, then selling, donating, giving
away, and trashing a lifetime of memories. I dreaded
it. As much as I didn't want to do it alone, I was glad
there wouldn't be anyone around so I could feel and cry
as intensely or gently as I wanted in private.

The overhead on our New York offices was steadily
increasing, and I continued to consider alternatives.
Everything in my life seemed to be pushing me into
isolation. I loved being a segment of this extended
family, but felt like a fraud knowing I'd be leaving
soon. I wondered how much of it was self-pity as I saw
myself an outsider looking in. Sitting on a boulder on
the beach, the water now looked like a polished mirror.
I wrapped my arms around my knees and was finally
strong enough to allow myself to think of my mother.

When I was a little girl, the State of New York
started cleaning up the sewage in the Hudson River.
My mom would take me for long walks along the

shoreline as it was being transformed into a thing of beauty. As I got older and needed alone time, I'd sit on a bench along the River. When I was done sitting or strolling, I always had the solution to any problem I was dealing with, even ones I hadn't known I'd been concerned about. My soul still yearned for the water. I would make it a point to carve out time to renew that habit, not only while I was here, but when I got back, as well.

Memories flooded me — childhood memories, memories of a woman loving me unconditionally no matter what circumstance I found myself in, always cheering, always devoted, never questioning, so proud of even my slightest accomplishment. She'd been instrumental in encouraging me to follow my dreams, and always was there to hold me when another emotionally unavailable male broke my heart when I recklessly believed I could change him. She'd selflessly given up her life to take care of her mother when it became evident Nana's mind was slipping.

Why wasn't I there for her more? Why didn't I tell her constantly how much I loved her? Why didn't I help ease her burden with Nana? My regrets came, not because I wasn't there, but because I wasn't aware of what was going on around me enough to think she might need support. I was so wrapped up in my world and what I was creating I didn't even know there was a life outside of my microcosm. Now it was too late to tell her. When the intense feelings of heartache came, when I missed her so much it stopped me in my tracks, the tears fell because I just hadn't known.

I accept that it will never be in my genetic makeup to be a full-time caregiver, and I have so much admiration for people like Miriam and Francine and Mama. I didn't beat myself up because I wasn't gifted in that area, I grieved because I could've made her life so much easier, and I didn't even show up the night she died like I'd promised because I was too busy holding a client's hand instead of the woman who loved me more than anyone else on earth. I couldn't change any of it now.

When I started sobbing, I was thankful. I had grieved briefly in Miles' arms the day I arrived, but right now I wanted to mourn my treasured mother, and in this gentle place with no one nearby, I rested my head on my knees and let the tears flow freely. I have no idea how long I was there, but I knew a certain release when I was cried out. I sat for a while, letting the calm breeze dry my tears. I felt her presence with me in a way I hadn't allowed myself before, and I was ready to start forgiving myself.

Feeling unburdened and refreshed, I wandered through town to the Manor, gray clouds now blanketing the earth. My heart skipped at the sight of Miles' truck in the driveway. Walking through the main room and not seeing signs of life, I called out, "Hell-ooo?"

"In The Library," he answered loud enough for me to hear.

"My, my, isn't *this* a nice surprise?" I asked, leaning against the doorframe of my room with arms crossed, watching Miles on a ladder.

"Hey, Jeni, good to see you, too," he laughed. "We changed out the light fixture recently so there'd be more light in here, but I didn't up the wattage on the bulbs. I thought you might like more reading light."

"Always the considerate Miles," I said, hearing my throatiness as I walked across the room and stood in front of him. His hands were occupied at the ceiling as my eyes devoured every delicious inch of him. I could see him getting harder, and, driven by some obscure impulse, my hands couldn't help but follow the path of my eyes, starting at his knees.

"What in the world are you doing, crazy woman?" he said, a growl in his voice as he grew visibly harder when my hands reached the top of his muscular thighs.

"Just enjoying the view," I said, bringing my face closer to his straining zipper, feeling my breathing getting more labored, right along with his. "I may come just watching you on that ladder."

"Jeni, don't start this," he said with a groan.

"Really? You serious you don't want this as much as I do? I've wanted it from the minute I laid eyes on you." I was cupping him with both hands now. He wasn't moving, but hardened with each pass over his manhood.

"Have you ever wondered why they call it a blow job?"

"What?" he asked, sounding like he was choking.

"I mean seriously, you're not blowing, you're sucking. Unless it refers to blowing the lid off, but I think of it more as exploding." I was trying to keep it light.

"Dear God, stop . . . We can't. And my hands are occupied," he said, strained enough I barely heard him.

"Good. Then you won't be able to stop me until you're done doing whatever it is you're doing." I slipped his zipper open, his magnificent erection popping free of its jeaned confines. "I've wanted to feel you against the back of my throat since we met. May I?" Not waiting for an answer, I wrapped my hands around him, my lips following close behind.

He was glorious, delicious, hard. When he started moving in and out of my mouth, I could feel how ready I was for him.

"Tell me you want this as much as I do." I looked up into his beautiful face.

"Of course I do, but you're leaving." His eyes met mine as his arms lowered. He tossed the forgotten bulb onto the mattress behind us, and cupped my chin with his now-empty hands. As I continued to suckle him, his fingers threaded through my hair, gently, then hard, then gently, keeping up with the age-old rhythm of my mouth.

"Who said anything about a relationship?" I smiled. "Listen, we've got today, Miles. Life is fragile, we both know it could be over tomorrow," I whispered. "I want you more in this moment than I've ever wanted anything in my life," I said as he came down from the stepladder.

"I don't want you for just a week," he said, taking me in his arms, his warmth and his hardness pressing into me. His eyes closed as his lips took mine. He lifted me, lips still together, wrapping my legs around his waist, the confines of my clothes acting as a barrier. I felt like a wild woman as powerful desire swept over me.

Sunrays piercing an overcast sky cast a peculiar, romantic sepia hue through the room. I wove my fingers through his hair, bringing his lips harder against mine. When he broke the kiss, I wanted more, but as he set me away from him, his hands on my shoulders, I felt lost. He turned away, he and his stunning erection, and headed for the door. I wondered how I would survive such rejection from a man with whom I felt such a kindred spirit, but my pride wouldn't allow me to beg him to stay as my chest grew heavy and my breathing labored.

When he reached the other side of the room, he hesitated as though making a decision. Looking back at me, he closed the door and locked it. I was afraid I might collapse from the sheer excitement of what that meant. I smiled as I held his gaze and slipped out of my jeans. He stopped mid-stride, his eyes caressing me as I lifted my shirt over my head. His arms were around me in a heartbeat, removing my bra, cupping my breasts, taking first one, then the other, into the warmth of his mouth. Delighting my lips again, I wasn't sure how long I could wait. When his finger entered me it fueled my desire, my knees grew weak, and I was desperate to remove his pants. Stepping out of them while not breaking eye contact, I knew I wasn't going to last long as he led me to the bed, pulled back the covers and lay down beside me.

Running his warm hand from my thigh to my throat, his golden eyes seemed to savor what they saw. "You're stunning," he whispered against my lips. "It was absurd to think I'd be able to resist you," his fingers opening me for exploration. He groaned, pressing harder as I reached for him, wrapping around him, pressing.

"You're deliciously wet," he said, sliding lower on the bed.

"I'm deliciously ready."

"That makes two of us." He pushed my knees open, then knelt, his hot breath licking my lower lips in exquisite ecstasy. His tongue started pressing in and out, slowly at first, then more intensely as my hips rose to give him greater access. I came hard and fast.

He kissed my thighs and ran his hands up my body, allowing me time to get my breathing under control. After a few minutes, he positioned himself above me, swollen, dripping. He entered me, pulled out, then entered me again. "You feel so good," he said in a guttural voice. "What are we doing, Jeni?" he asked, strained.

"Living for the moment."

His rhythm grew harder, faster, filling me deeper. My nails raked his powerful back, my desire for him overwhelming. His strokes became slower. I watched him moving over me, his neck taut as he brought me to the brink again, slowed, then thrust deep. His lips took mine, tongues dueling. I grabbed his hips and held him closer, harder, all the while kissing him with the same pattern, throbbing with his rhythm, memorizing his face that was so dear to me.

As I raised my hips to meet him thrust for thrust, breath accelerated, I grasped the bedding as he found the exact spot. When our lips met in one last crescendo, we peaked together, a current of life flowing through him, his warm release a surprising turn-on to my already-engaged heart. Moments passed as we lay with foreheads together as our breathing quieted.

He rolled languidly to his back, taking me with him. Wrapped in his arms, head on his chest, I said quietly, "That was incredible."

He kissed me softly. "I don't do one-night-stands, Jeni."

"Thank God. I'd hate to think that was the only time I could experience such an earth-shattering event."

"From the day I met you, I've wanted you like no other. But you're just passing through. 'Love 'em and leave 'em' doesn't work in my life, it can't. I have a strong attachment to you, to Nana. But if my heart gets involved and you go away, that leaves a big part of me empty."

"I'll be back often."

"It's not enough, not for me."

"Can't we see where it takes us over the next week or so? Enjoy this indescribable attachment we have? Do *that* again?" I smiled and kissed his chest.

He wrapped me in his arms, nestling me in an embrace, kissing my hair.

"I don't know how much I can let go, so I'm telling you now, when the time comes, I'll walk away while I still can."

"Deal. I promise, you won't be sorry."

Cocooned against each other, we talked about life. About his mother's recent death and how hard it had been on him to take months off work to take care of her because she deserved that much from her only son.

About the house she left him in Sugarloaf. We talked about my walk along the shoreline today and how different it was to lose a mother unexpectedly, with no warning, and how neither was preferable.

We headed to the kitchen to throw a meal together, talking the whole while. We talked about Nana, her care, and the home my mother left me in Brooklyn. How both our mothers had the foresight to have life insurance, and how, even in death, they continued to take care of their children.

As much as I wanted him to stay, he insisted he needed to leave. There would be guests in two rooms tomorrow, and he would check in on his way home, see if I needed help. His goodnight kiss was poignant. The day had been exhausting. I was asleep immediately.

Putting the finishing touches on the suites the next morning, I hummed cheerful tunes. I had meals planned for tomorrow and the following day, the rooms were ready, there were fresh flowers in the dining room and fruit and chocolates in the rooms. What a charming diversion it was to be here. Still early, I brought my computer to the kitchen and wrote ad copy for one of our projects. Inspiration flowed in new ways, and I knew what I'd written was better than anything I'd done in a while. Nothing like a little sex to get the creative juices flowing, I thought, permitting myself delicious memories throughout the day.

CHAPTER SEVEN

Miles. There was a grace about him, sensitive with no threat to his manhood, profoundly fond of an aging woman whose mind deteriorated daily, masterful in bed. I colored with pleasure as I remembered yesterday.

The smile was still on my face when I poked my head into the cottage. "Good morning, Janet," Nana said from the overstuffed recliner with the sunshine pouring in around her. "You look well rested." I had learned not to correct her no matter who she thought I was, but tried as much as possible to be who she needed at any given moment.

Miles had given me great advice about the two worlds I'd have to switch between. One would be *our* world, those of us who still maintained some semblance of our intelligence and rational thought. But if we understood those with dementia do not occupy that world, then we could consciously take a step, a physical step if need be, to the left or right to make us aware we were entering *their* world. Life would be easier for everyone. That way, the things that bother us in our world would have no power to affect us because we would be thinking on a different plane. Like the sixth time in five minutes when she asks what time it is, or when is Henry going to be home? His suggestion had helped me many times to be more understanding and patient.

She stood in front of the grandfather clock and opened the glass door in a surprisingly gentle manner as she removed the key from the wall. Winding the clock that was probably a century old, Nana said, "Henry and I were talking about your teacher this morning. I'm not sure she's challenging you enough. Henry wants me to look into special classes for you that will develop some of your artistic talent that doesn't get used nearly as much as it should."

"I'd love that, Mama," I said, smiling at Miriam. They must have countless conversations that jump from one topic to another, few of which were based in present-day reality. It took a special calling to do what Miriam was doing, and she did it wonderfully.

"Francine will be here this afternoon," Miriam said. "I'm going to do some shopping, take care of a few items of business I need to catch up on."

"Let me know if there's anything I can do to help. We have guests tonight and everything's ready, so I'll have free time."

"Thanks for the offer. I'm looking forward to wandering mindlessly for a while," she said.

"I can only imagine . . . no, actually I can't imagine. You have a true gift."

"We all have a calling. It's a blessing when we get to use it."

"Love how I stop breathing for a second every time I see you," I said to Miles when he dropped by that evening.

"Love how you say whatever's on your mind. It's kinda fun to have no idea what words will come out of your mouth."

"And it's kinda fun the things I *do* with my mouth, huh?" I was sure we both had a vision of the ladder in mind.

After hesitating, he shook his head and said, "That was more than 'kinda fun.' That was . . ."

"What was it?" I asked, stepping up to him and putting my arms around his waist.

He ran his fingers through my hair. "It was a fantasy fulfillment," he said huskily. "Found it hard to concentrate today."

"Oh, I love it when that happens!" I said, rising on tiptoe to capture his lips. "And I'm so glad it wasn't just me."

"No, it wasn't just you. There were two of us involved."

His words pleased me. He pleased me. "We'll have to do it again soon," I said. "And often."

He didn't respond, just kept looking at me. He licked his lips in an intimate way. "Cinnamon?"

"Yep, fresh rolls waiting for morning mouths to devour them," I said suggestively.

"I bet it would look good spread, sweet to the taste," he said in a husky voice. "The cinnamon, I mean."

Did he have the same vision I did, lapping cinnamon from naughty places? The butter knife fell from my limp fingers and clanged to the hard floor. There were unspoken words lying deep in his eyes as he leaned slowly to pick it up. Starting at my ankles, he drew the knife deliberately over my jeans to my knee, over my thigh, ending at the peak between my legs.

"You need anything? You have everything ready for breakfast?" His voice was strained.

I opened my eyes. "Breakfast? Oh, yes, two very nice couples checked in," I said, chest rising with my strained breaths. "But I've got a lot of confidence in my cooking abilities, so I'll be fine. I'm doing something simple, just Almond Crusted French Toast with berries and roasted apples. Want to stay for dinner – or something?"

"Thanks, but I gotta get home."

"Can I . . . ? Will you . . . ? Maybe we can . . ."

"Is your brain going faster than your mouth can keep pace with?" he asked with a smile lurking on his face. "That's remarkable, since your mouth can keep up with almost anything. How's Nana?"

I laughed out loud, coming back to a semblance of reality. "She's having a good day. Francine's here, Miriam took a break, and you never know where the conversation's going to lead. Talk about no filter."

"Was she that way before?"

"Not at all," I said, remembering the prim and proper grandmother of my youth. "I was shocked initially the night she took her shirt off in a bar, but from what I've found out, that's pretty common. Makes me wonder what part of the brain dementia is activating."

"Wondering if yours is already activated?" he asked, stepping out of my reach as I understood his joke.

"If I'm like this now, I'd hate to see what I'd be like if I really didn't have a filter. Speaking of which," I said, "when are you coming back?"

"Tomorrow if you need me."

"No, I mean, when are you gonna come and stay? Overnight, like a slumber party."

"Jeni, Jeni, Jeni, what am I gonna do with you?"

Staring at the front of his pants that seemed to react to my visual stimulus, I asked, "Well, I wasn't thinking of a pillow fight, but would you like for me to explain in minute detail what I'd *like* for you to do?"

"I think my imagination can take care of that, thanks," he said in a low voice as I stood toe to toe with him, rubbing his growing erection. "God, you push me to the brink."

"I know. Isn't it fun how we can turn each other on with just a look or a word?"

"I'm nuts to even suggest it, but how about Friday? You've got guests tomorrow and they'll be gone Friday morning. Anyone checking in this weekend?"

"No, just me, all alone in this big ol' house. Whatever am I to do?"

"I'll bring cards, we'll play Canasta."

Serving the guests had been enjoyable, non-stressful, and somehow satisfying. I could understand how Jordan had been willing to give up her high-powered New York job in her father's law firm for the love of a good man and a Victorian mansion she had equipped with modern-day conveniences. I'm not sure I'd want to do it all the time, but she had the staff to find a balance between the enjoyable parts and the tediousness of routine.

When the chores were done, I hung up my apron, packed my computer in my backpack, and checked in on Francine and Nana.

"What are those?" Nana asked.

"What are what?" I asked, not understanding her question.

She got up and walked over to the table and picked up my keys. "What's this?" she asked.

It was all I could do not to break down when I looked at Francine. "They open doors for you," I said, knowing by the look on her face she had no idea what I was talking about.

My walk into town was no longer as carefree as when I'd left the Manor. The Blue Owl bookstore is across the street from the Carousel of Happiness. Feeling sad, I popped in for a cup of coffee and to catch up on some correspondence. As with most places in this little community, the owner and patrons were friendly, and it was almost two hours before I was heading back.

"Give you a ride, stranger?" Miles said, pulling up to the curb. "I was up at Jack's place and saw you come out. Enjoying yourself?"

"Even more so now." I smiled as he leaned over and opened the door for me.

"Where to?"

"Just back to the Manor, thanks. Can't believe how tired I am, and I got a good night's sleep."

"Lots of water, take it easy for a while. Sounds like it may still be altitude – or a lack of exercise."

My bark of laughter was immediately followed by a yawn.

It only took a minute to make it back. "We still on for tomorrow night?" I asked. Did I really blush?

"Looking forward to it," he said. "I'll bring some of my world famous spaghetti and we can cook in Jordan's extraordinary kitchen."

"It is, isn't it? Sometimes when I'm in there I think of the first time I saw you." There was that blush again.

"Yeah, I've thought of that day more than a time or two," he said, kissing me on the cheek and opening the door. "Now, skedaddle, I have work to do."

"We could make it quick."

"Get out, now, before I take you up on it. We have tomorrow night and I'm late as it is."

"Be that way," I said. "Tomorrow it is then. I'll make dessert. Thanks for the ride."

"The ride . . . my pleasure, I assure you."

Even enfolded in this tranquil atmosphere, impending New York life was rearing its ugly head, intruding on the calm of my surroundings. The client I had worked so hard to land was pushing for a meeting, and while I knew my time here was short, I couldn't seem to find the desire to rush back and hold their hand. I was keeping them apprised of our progress on their campaign, and they were encouraging in their apparent appreciation of the ad design, meeting with my staff, but seemed to feel one-on-one time with me was a necessity. I had Skyped with them a few days ago, but that didn't seem to be enough. I was conflicted about what I was even looking for anymore.

The introspection was beneficial and my pace was slower than it'd been in years. I thought about what I was looking for in life, knowing I wouldn't just snap my fingers and have the answers, but at least I was slowing down enough to think. Not for the first time, I wondered if Jordan was truly happy having left a high-powered law practice in the City for the quiet mountain solitude of Nederland. I didn't know if I could do it.

Pulling myself out of my reflective reverie, I was eager to crack down and be creative. The guests would check out early in the morning. I had their breakfast of buttermilk crepes with raspberry and yogurt filling ready, laundry was done, and work around the Manor was finished. Thoughts of tomorrow night pushed their way into my imagination with anticipation, but it was time to buckle down and be productive. My inspiration was in overdrive and fresh ideas were flowing. I was immensely pleased with the progress I was making and how this particular campaign was coming together.

The intercom buzzed. "Have you seen your grandmother?" a rather frantic Francine asked.

"No, I've been buried in paperwork. Let me look around." Somehow I wasn't surprised to find her in the kitchen going through the refrigerator.

Leaning against the doorframe, I asked, "Can I help you?" She didn't even seem startled, just gave me a cursory glance and asked why I didn't have any ice cream for her.

"How'd you get here, Nana?" I asked gently.

"How do you think? I walked," she said, matter-of-factly, not slowing down from rearranging the freezer. "None of this even looks like it's worth taking up space, much less going to the trouble of eating it."

"How did you get in the house?" I asked again, trying to figure out how to keep a better eye on her. I'd have to remember to ask Miles if we could set up a camera in the cottage.

"I came through the door, how do you think I got in? Now stop asking such foolish questions and take me to get some ice cream."

"Francine?" I said into the intercom.

"Did you find her?" said an anxious voice on the other end.

"Yes, she's here. I'm going to take her to get some ice cream. I'll have her back in an hour or so."

"Oh, thank God. I'm so sorry, Jeni. She was here one minute and gone the next. I never even heard the door close." I remembered Miles telling me they could be creative when they decided they wanted to get somewhere.

"Not a problem. We'll figure it out."

"Thank you. Again, I'm sorry."

The ever-charming Sam at the Amber Rose was glad to see us. Nana seemed to think of him as an old friend, and he played right along.

"Haven't seen you in a coon's age, Elizabeth. Where you been keeping yourself?" he said, winking at me.

"They try to keep me locked up like a prisoner, Sam." We exchanged a smile because she'd remembered his name. "But it doesn't matter what they do. I have them outsmarted and can leave whenever I want."

Sensing it was somehow important, I asked, "How do you outsmart them, Elizabeth?"

"If I told you, it wouldn't be a secret anymore, now would it? I'm not having them clip my wings, and I'm not telling tales out of school. Just mind your own business and I'll take care of myself."

Knowing it was useless to argue when she was in this frame of mind, I asked Sam if he had any ice cream. "Got some in this morning. What kind would you like?"

"Something with nuts and chocolate," she was quick to respond.

He was serving her in no time, and the delighted look of satisfaction that crossed her face as she took the first bite was endearing.

"Janet never wants me to have nuts," she said, reverting again.

"That's because she's trying to save those old teeth of yours," Sam said affectionately.

"Old? Speak for yourself. I've had this set of teeth since kindergarten, and forty years isn't asking too much out of them. They should last me at least another forty years," she said with some authority.

I loved how Sam rolled with the punches, and whatever era she found herself in, he was right there with her.

"You sure are a little thing," Sam said with affection.

"I may be little, but I'm mighty," she said matter-of-factly, causing an immediate laugh from both of us.

When she was finished, she got up and walked out. Sam and I smiled at each other. "I guess that means she's done."

"Appears that way," I said, throwing some bills on the counter and racing out the door after Nana.

"Where you going in such a hurry?" I asked, out of breath as I came up behind her as she rushed toward the water.

CHAPTER EIGHT

"She's dead, isn't she?" she cried as she continued on.

Understanding what she was asking, I said, "Yes, Nana. She is."

"Did I kill her?"

"*What*? What on earth do you mean?"

As she approached the water's edge, she turned to me with tears standing in her eyes. "Is she dead because of me?"

"Oh, sweetheart, no! Of course not. She had a bad heart valve that none of us knew about. She died peacefully in her sleep. There was nothing you nor I nor anyone else could have done to prevent it."

"How will I live without her?"

"I know it's not the same, but I'm here. You have Miriam and Francine, and you're happy here."

"But you're leaving and I'll be alone again." Her words devastated me, and I let out a ragged sob. She was aware I was leaving, and the only family she had ever known would be gone.

In a voice choked with tears I said, "You won't be alone. You'll be surrounded by people who love and care for you."

She turned to walk toward the Manor. "James Gabriel will be coming soon. We need to get back."

I took her hand and we walked in silence for a few minutes. "I love you so much, Nana. I'm sorry you're hurting."

"Hurting about what? Of course you love me, you've always been a good daughter."

She was gone again. Glimpses of the woman trapped inside the body were becoming fewer and fewer, but nonetheless poignant.

As predicted, James Gabriel was waiting for her when we arrived. "There's my boy," she said with a smile. She seemed to always be aware of who he was. "Ready for more stories?"

"Sure am," he said excitedly. "Mama even let me bring my knife so I can whittle while you tell me about some of the things you did when you were a kid like me."

I headed back to the house, feeling the burden of leaving her to the care of others. Jordan and Brandan would be back Sunday, and all too soon I'd be heading to New York, at odds with myself.

The butterflies were making a valiant effort to be released from my chest at the thought of the approaching evening. I'd been with other men over the years, but none of them had touched my core the way Miles did. From the moment we met several months ago, it had been an intense attraction, physical and emotional, the likes of which I'd never experienced. Thinking about spending a night with him had me twitter-pated.

When he walked in the back door at dinnertime, his roguish eyes sparkled with hundreds of small fires. His face was compelling, and while not classically handsome, his looks spoke to every cell in my body. He carried two grocery sacks and had a bouquet of flowers.

Tears – where did the tears keep coming from? His lips twitched with compassionate amusement. "Whatever is the matter? Did you forget I was coming?"

"Not something I'd likely forget, silly. You catch me off guard with your thoughtfulness," I said, taking the flowers from his hand. "Oh, they are for me, aren't they?"

"Now who's being silly?" he said, setting the bags on the polished countertop and drawing me close as he kissed my forehead. I tilted my head to offer my lips in invitation. I didn't have to ask twice. Without breaking contact, he took the flowers and set them next to the bags, wrapping me in his arms, bringing me to intimate proximity with his hardness.

"I've thought of little else all day."

"That makes two of us," I said, again drawing him to me. A clock ticked in the distance as our tongues played a mating game and hands roamed the other's body. I heard the moaning sounds coming from me. "It takes nothing for you to make me uninhibited."

"I know. It's an attractive trait." His mouth twisted in a teasing smile, "But we have all night." He opened one of the bags and began removing items. "Miles' world famous spaghetti sauce," he said, setting a large jar on the counter. "Angel hair pasta . . . garlic bread . . . and a blend of Merlot/Cab/Shiraz." He set a unique bottle on the counter.

"Looks like you lived up to your end of the bargain," I said, opening the oven to check on the pie that was almost finished. "I wasn't sure which kind you'd like, so I made my to-die-for pecan, and a fresh apple pie made with apples from Jordan's tree. And I found some homemade vanilla ice cream in the deep freeze, so that particular appetite should be well-sated by the time the evening is over."

"Just one of the appetites I intend to take care of tonight, if I can wait that long." He slipped the pencil from the twist in my hair and let it cascade to my shoulders. "I love how you do that to your hair. It's so you."

"There's no particular order of business for this encounter. We don't have to wait."

"I'm hot from a long day of work, so when the time comes, maybe we can take a shower. You know, to clean up from the exertion of eating and all," he said with a devilish grin.

"Yeah, I think we can make that happen."

The food, the kisses, the wine, the kisses, the dessert, the kisses . . . it was perfection. But nothing compared to the company. The passion flared again as we finished cleaning the kitchen. "What exactly is it about you that obsesses me?" he asked.

"Maybe the taste of dinner on her lips?" Nana said from behind us.

We both jumped, and were even more startled at the sound of knocking on the back door.

"What the . . ." I said, somewhat perturbed.

Francine was in her robe, panting from a run from the cottage. "I'm so sorry, Jeni. I set the alarm before I hopped in the shower. I'll have to have you check it sometime to see why it didn't work," she said, stepping into the kitchen. Not exactly how I had the evening planned, but Miles, always the gentleman, was offering Nana some pecan pie.

"Of course I want some," she said, almost batting her eyes at him. "It's probably not as good as the pie I make, but I'd love to try yours."

"I used your recipe, Nana, it will be pretty similar."

"Have we met?" she asked, taking a seat at the counter.

"Might as well make yourself at home, Francine. Looks like it'll be a while."

Once I got past my frustration, we had an enjoyable time. Nana told stories of younger years that were accurate to my memory. The fragility of the mind continued to cause me to wonder how some memories could stay intact, but not allow her to remember her own granddaughter, or the death of her daughter, or what she'd just eaten. It was a puzzle.

It was almost an hour later when they left. The dishwasher was running. "Did you put the candlesticks away?" I asked, looking in the cupboard where Jordan normally kept them.

"No, I haven't noticed them since you blew them out, and the only reason I noticed them then is because I was watching your mouth."

"Oh, I like the way you think. But that's strange. I set them by the sink to clean off the wax before I put them away, and then I don't remember seeing them again. Oh, well," I set the dish towel on the rack. "Still up for this?"

"Is that a loaded question?" he asked, locking and chaining the door.

"Is it a loaded answer?" I sassed. He hung his head with a smirk and got a lopsided smile. Extending his hand as he turned out the lights, he said, "Let's go find out."

The shower in The Library, the main floor suite, was done in pleasing terra cotta tiles and blended with the overall masculine feeling of the decor. The room was steaming by the time we'd removed our clothes, and I was ready to explode at his touch. Both showerheads were on, and we adjusted them to hit in just the right place on each other's back. Hot water sluiced over each of us as we fondled and kissed and stroked with wet abandon. His tongue kept rhythm with his thrusting finger. I wanted more as the moistness he was feeling between my legs had nothing to do with the spray of the shower.

I wanted him deeper, wanted him inside me. The way the water was hitting our backs was perfection, keeping us warm with an occasional spray over the shoulder. He moved harder, and I raised my leg, inviting his thrusts. I held him in one hand, the other hand braced against the wall, standing on tiptoe on one foot to guide him. I was close to desperate. As he entered me, he lifted me slightly. I wrapped my arms around him, kissing him with reckless abandon, feeling the pulse in every nerve ending. With a sudden, startled cry, he swung me toward the wall, protecting my head with his hand and covering me with his taught-muscled body.

"What . . . in the world . . ." I tried to figure out what caused the end of our reality so quickly.

"Your . . . foot . . ." He was gasping for air, head against mine when rumbling laughter took hold of him. When his amusement mellowed and his breathing became not quite so labored, he said, "When I was a kid, a stray came into our yard to mate with our dog who was in heat. My grandfather threw a bucket of ice water them. That entire concept just became crystal clear."

"What?"

"Your foot, it hit the handle and turned the water frigid in an instant. Not at all what I was expecting, especially in the, um, shall we say, heat of the moment."

When it registered what he was telling me, I looked at the handle that was now pointing downward. "Oh, my God, I'm *sooo* sorry!"

"I'm sure it was just as shocking for you," he said, adjusting the handle back to a warm position. "But if you don't mind, why don't we warm up and get out of here?"

"Oh, Miles," I said, covering my mouth with both hands, torn between embarrassment and hysterical laughter. Laughter won out and continued until we were drying off.

"Nothing like ice water to make you limp in an instant," he said, running the towel over his head, standing in all of his naked glory.

"I can't believe I'm going to say this, but I'm almost afraid to try again."

He stopped rubbing his hair and said, "You don't strike me as timid. I say, third time's a charm and we should figure out how to be charming."

"You sure about that? It's been a pretty disjointed evening so far."

"But it's all been fun - and memorable. I got a chill in my bones that the warm water didn't seem to ease. I'm all for hopping in that huge bed, sharing body heat in the center of it, holding each other close, and, at the very least, sharing stories."

"At the very least," I assured him. "But I agree, let's grab some wine and a snack, lock the door, get under the covers, and warm each other up."

Jordan had spared no expense setting up the suites and the bedding, and this room was no exception. The king-sized bed was inviting and luxurious. Shoulder to shoulder, we ate cheese and grapes and drank wine. Our time together was intimate. We were completely comfortable in our glorious nakedness as we shared stories that deepened our growing friendship.

"Do you ever feel guilty?" I asked quietly.

"It's too easy to second guess the 'what ifs,' so it's not a concept I like to embrace, but what were you specifically asking about?"

"I feel guilty about my mom all the time. The things I didn't say, the time I didn't spend with her, the times I should've told her I loved her that I just let slip by. All she ever did was love me, and I didn't even keep my promise to her the night she died."

"What promise was that?"

"I hadn't been there all week. I'd been working to secure this international beverage company for their ad campaign and I was working eighteen-hour days. I promised her that particular night would be different and I'd be there in time for dinner. She must have died a few hours after dinner. I found Nana in bed with her the next morning, my mother cold as ice."

"What was she doing in bed with her?"

"Trying to warm her up. And I keep thinking of that moment when I realized she was dead. In my finite world, it never occurred to me my mother could die, that she wouldn't always be there. It was such a paradigm shift in my life."

"And now you realize the things you thought were so important don't matter nearly as much?"

"That's so true. The client I thought was the most important thing in my world is a constant strain, and I'm often overwhelmed I spent so much time on the phone with him that night and didn't get a chance to tell my mother goodbye."

"What you're going through is a natural part of grief. You have a double-whammy with Nana, but I'm glad you've had down time here to help you deal with it. It'll get easier, and in time you will realize you did everything you could with the information you had available to you at the time."

"Is that how it was for you?"

"Mine was so different. I had time with her. I knew she was going to die. I got to say all the things I ever wanted to say. I got to love on her and wait on her, and give her back at least a small portion of what she had given me when she was a young widow all those years ago. My regrets were different, but there's no doubt the time I had with her changed the way I've lived my life since then."

He set the goblets and plate on the bedside table and turned out the antique brass reading light. We snuggled under the covers with his arms around me, my head on his chest. "What regrets do you have?" I asked softly.

"That's for a later discussion. Suffice it to say, her death was just another of the many lessons she taught me in her lifetime. She was a dynamic and strong woman who wanted desperately to live. If nothing else, I try to focus on thoroughly living each day, living in the moment. I appreciate the people and things around me and use my words as much as possible so when it's time for me to leave this world, not one of the people I love will ever doubt how I felt about them."

I wanted to be one of the people who heard those words. I ached with how much this man meant to me, how much respect I had for him, his compassion, his quiet strength, his love and care for those around him. I knew in my heart he wasn't for me. I would be leaving soon, and I was trying to cheat fate to take from him what I could in the short time we had left.

CHAPTER NINE

Somewhere in the middle of a tender and poignant dream, his lips on my breast woke me. The flat of his tongue hardened my nipple, and I arched my back to get closer.

"Is this what they call a wet dream?" I chuckled groggily. "Please don't wake me."

"No dream. Just one man wanting one woman to the point of distraction."

With eyes closed and a soft sigh forming in my throat, the clean, masculine scent of him was part of the aura he created around us. As his tongue circled one swollen breast and then the other, his gentle but calloused hand lowered to the flat of my stomach. "I want you so much I ache," he said. "I wake at night wanting you. I can't believe you're here in my arms, warm, soft, delicate, wanting me the same way."

His voice was deep, raspy, and set me aflame. I lifted my hips in invitation for him to explore lower. I didn't have to ask twice. His hand cupped my mound before his finger split my lips to find the throbbing heat waiting inside for him. Two fingers entered me, grabbing the moistness to tease my raindrop nub which seemed to have grown a pulse of its own. In and out, just enough pressure to bring me to the brink, then he'd enter me again. His arousal was evident in his eyes. "Spread your thighs for me, I want to rub my tongue over you."

His words fueled me. I lifted my knees, spreading them in invitation. Rolling to situate himself between my legs, he never broke eye contact. With hands on my hips, he backed up until he was kneeling on the floor, pulling me to the edge of the bed. I drew a pillow down to put under my head so I could watch what he was doing. He put my legs over his shoulders, keeping eye contact until the time his tongue found my sweet spot. Then neither of us was watching, just feeling. His excitement was a turn on, and my body was reacting in delicious new ways.

His hot tongue slid over me, gently then hard, sending shots of raw ecstasy through my limbs as I used his shoulders to lift myself closer and closer to his pursuing mouth. When his fingers entered me, my climax exploded at the intense pleasure he caused. He suckled gently as the aftershocks rocked my body, and the boyish grin of satisfaction that crossed his face was captivating.

Standing, I was impressed with his thick, hard manhood that stood between us. The thought processed that the body was a fascinating instrument that I could stretch to accommodate his size. Rolling over, I took my pillow and myself to the head of the bed, lying on my stomach, feeling his weight on the mattress as he straddled my hips. "You're as flawless as the heart of a diamond," he said, almost in a whisper, as his strong hands cupped my hips, and stroked up and down the muscles of my back. He lifted my hips in the air until I was on my knees, and teased my wet opening with just his tip.

Wanting more, I began pressing against him to take him deeper where his tongue had just been, inch by glorious inch, in and out in a sensual tempo. With one hand on my hip, he continued to rock me. The other hand gave just the right amount of pressure to my aching need. I could feel the ridges of his rim moving in and out, and the combined pressure had me grinding against him harder, wilder, until I could feel my burst of pleasure, milking him as his muscles tensed, trembling inside me, spilling his liquid heat in an explosion of pure gratification.

He continued to run his hands over my back. Rolling over, he enfolded me in his arms, my head resting against his chest, and touched me with sweet affection in the warm aftermath of intimacy. For the first time, I understood what the word lovemaking meant.

"Is there a description for what we do to each other?" he asked, running his fingers through my hair, loosening the knots.

"Even I can't think of a word to sufficiently describe it," I said with a yawn, "but I'll be glad to sleep on it and get back to you in the morning with what I figure out."

He stroked me, kissing me gently on the forehead. My last conscious thought was that I could get used to this.

It was 6:45 the following morning when Jordan's familiar ring woke me.

"Good morning?" I said, trying to gain some semblance of consciousness.

"Oh, I'm so sorry, I didn't mean to wake you. I forgot the time difference."

"Not a problem, sweetheart. You know you can call me any time. What's up?"

Miles curled up behind me and pulled me close to a spooning position, kissing my shoulder.

"We'll be home around noon tomorrow. Father is doing so much better and there's no need for us to stay, so we're catching an early flight."

"I can't wait to see you. Everything will be ready for your arrival."

"How *are* things? How's Nana?"

"Nana seems to be doing well. Miriam and Francine are perfect nurse/companions, and things couldn't be more enjoyable."

"And Miles?"

"What about Miles?" I asked, wondering if she would hear the breathlessness in my voice as his tongue found its way up my neck.

"Don't be coy with me, young lady. I've known you for almost two decades. So tell me . . ."

"Why don't we talk about it when you get back tomorrow? I'll fix one of my specialty dishes, we'll have some wine and relax with an early Sunday dinner and I'll fill you in then."

"Is he *there*?"

"Is who here?" I laughed.

"Oh, girlie, you got some tales to tell. How long will you stay?"

"I'll get a flight out early Monday. I have to get back. The little brats at work aren't doing well with their babysitter, and I have to get home and whip them back into shape."

"Can't wait to see you. You can fill me in when we get there."

"Will do. Give Riley and Patricia my love, and give your brute of a husband a big smooch for me."

"Trust me, that won't be an effort. Love you, Jeni. Take care of yourself."

"I'm on it. Love you, too. See you tomorrow."

When I rolled over, Miles was not only no longer in bed, he was dressed and brushing his hair in the bathroom. I put my arms around his waist. "Got a date?" I asked, teasing because I was a little disappointed he wasn't ready to play anymore.

"Got a bunch of errands I need to run and have some small jobs to finish. I need to get out of here." He seemed a cold and indifferent stranger.

I was stung and more than a little hurt by his manner, concentrating a lot harder than was necessary on tying the belt of my robe. "I was hoping we could spend the day together." *Don't whine, Jeni*, I told myself, *you don't need to beg.*

"Sorry, I've got things to do."

"Do you want some company?" *Dammit, why did I ask that?*

"No, another body along will just complicate things."

"You didn't seem to think so last night." *What the hell was the matter with me? Let him go, stop trying to hold on when he's clearly trying to run away.*

He stopped as he was walking out of the room. Touching my face, he ran the back of his fingers gently across my cheek. "No, Jeni, last night was breathtaking, all of it. I won't let you believe otherwise. But I let myself forget for a moment that another body is a serious complication, a complication I can't afford in my life. It won't happen again."

"Please," I said.

"You're leaving. I broke my own rule, and for that I take full responsibility and apologize. I don't need or want a one-night stand. My life isn't set up for a part-time affair. I'm sorry if I led you to believe otherwise."

"You warned me on more than one occasion. I was willing to take the risk," I said, not caring to stop the silent tears.

"We have something undeniable between us, but it's not enough. I like you more than I would have believed possible. I wish you nothing but the best and I'll watch out for Nana as much as I can." He kissed me softly on the lips and was gone.

The door closed behind him. I'd chosen unwisely in the past, was aware the men I'd known were not worth keeping, and I'd often wondered if that was the reason I chose them, because I didn't want anyone sticking around. But Miles – everything about him was different, distinctive, desirable.

The ache was a gripping pain like tentacles wrapping themselves around my heart, squeezing. For a moment I'd begun to consider our possibilities, even started to believe them. My broken spirit needed to accept that I was hoping for someone else's happily-ever-after. I wasn't a forever kind of girl, I thought as I choked back a sob.

Needing to keep myself distracted, I made sure everything was clean, all the sheets and towels washed, and all the ingredients ready for tomorrow's dinner. Knowing I didn't have much time left to spend with her, but not knowing if she would even be aware of who I was, I wandered to the cottage. Miriam answered my knock as Nana was cleaning the glass on the grandfather clock, talking to my grandfather.

"You know you can't do that anymore, Henry," she said. Miriam smiled and went back to the kitchen.

"Oh, Mary Beth," Nana said to me, "Henry insists on jumping out and scaring me. I dropped my teacup the last time, but he won't listen. He thinks it's such a fun game."

I had no idea who Mary Beth was, but it didn't matter. "I'm sure he'll stop doing it if you just ignore him, Elizabeth."

"Elizabeth? I've been Betty since the day we met. Since when have you been so formal as to call me Elizabeth? And how do you expect me to ignore him when he scares me every time I come around the corner?"

"Boys will be boys," I said, trying to improvise. "Besides, when they tease like that it usually means they like you."

She turned, studying me for a moment, then sat in her chair in front of the fire. "I can't seem to get warm," she said, pulling a shawl around her shoulders.

"A bath always helps me get warm," I suggested.

Again she stared at me. "Go home now. I'll take a bath as you suggest. Come back tomorrow." She was gone, and I was uncertain. How had my mother done it for so long? Seeing the figure of someone you've always loved, but knowing they, as you knew them, no longer inhabited the shell.

Callie and Charlotte Rose were pulling into the driveway. I was pleased to see them. The last thing I wanted was to be alone right now.

"To what do I owe this pleasure?" I asked as I opened the back door to a smiling child.

"We were on our way home and wanted to see if you've heard anything from Jordan."

"Is it all right if I get her out of her car seat?" Charlotte Rose had her arms extended eagerly for her anticipated escape.

"Sure. I can't stay long, but we're just coming back from Denver, and she's ready to be free."

"Come on in, I'll fix us some tea." I led the way, nuzzling this precious child, overwhelmed with the circle of life, pulling myself away from getting lost in the dark thoughts of life's beautiful beginning, its promise, and its unexpected twists.

"I'm so glad you stopped by. Jordan and Brandan come home tomorrow and I'll be leaving the next day." Why did the thought of that cause my heart to clench? "My mom left me her house in Brooklyn. When I get back, I have to sort through her things, then sell it. I thought maybe you could refer me to a good Realtor there."

"Of course I can. I have a great network of resources, and we'll find one who specializes in your area."

"I'd appreciate that. Just the thought of it is overwhelming."

"I'll do everything I can to help from this end," she said, touching my arm. "I can advise you on getting it clutter free, then have someone help you get it staged, if you'd like. We'll make it as painless as possible."

I opened the cupboard door with the pots and pans and set Charlotte Rose in front of it, hoping to keep her occupied for a few minutes. Callie and I talked, some about the process, about the business aspect of it, and the emotional turmoil in front of me.

"When my mother died," Callie said, "I had my father to help clear her things out. It was one of the hardest parts of the entire process. I don't know what I would have done without him. Do you at least have someone to help you?"

"If I need someone, I'll have someone there. Right now it feels like I'd rather do it alone so I have the ability to cry, or take my time to look through things, or not look and just toss."

"Don't feel it's a sign of weakness if you need help," she said. "I found it was a lot harder when I was alone. I wanted to read every single piece of paper. That's not the goal right now. Your objective will be to clear out what needs to be gone. As you have time over the months, you can go through each paper you kept in a box, see what's important to you, what's not."

"Thank you," I said, squeezing her hand. "I know it has to be done, I'm just dreading it."

"Of course you are. The sooner you get it done, the better. And I know people who can help with that, also, so don't hesitate to ask."

"That takes a huge burden off me, thanks. The only time I've been back since she died was to get Nana's clothes. It was awful. Sometimes I wish I didn't have to go back at all."

"Hopefully, like I did, you'll find a new peace when you think of her, and a new beginning to healing."

With pans clattering in the background from a delighted Charlotte Rose, Callie and I talked. She told me briefly about running away to her father's cabin here in Nederland to escape the stalker who tried to kill her, and how she met Jack and Sam at the Amber Rose the first day she came to town. She was smitten from that day on.

She and Jack own several houses around the state, but they spend the bulk of their time between Denver and Nederland. She still sells real estate from her Boulder office, but she's slowed down a lot since Charlotte Rose was born. We even talked about an ad campaign for her business, something I'd love to design for her. The people in this quaint town take care of their own. Torn between needing to go back and not wanting to leave, I felt as though I was being swung over an ocean, and someone was going to let go of me to fly out over the deep end to flounder on my own.

As we said our good-byes at the car, I invited her for dinner the following evening, a last supper, of sorts. I was leaving a lot of me behind, and I wanted to make it as special as possible. I couldn't wait to see Jordan and hear about their trip, about Wiley Riley, her powerful but tender father, and to be together one last time for a while.

CHAPTER TEN

The tears falling on my pillow weren't for any reason other than self-pity. I couldn't take care of Nana myself, I knew that, but I wouldn't even be near her. I argued with myself constantly about whether or not it mattered if she didn't know who I was. As time progressed, I knew she'd need more care. Facing the sale of Mama's house was also weighing heavily on me. There was such a finality to it, but even more so in sorting through her possessions. I dreaded opening that particular wound, and had apprehension about how I'd be able to heal it once it was opened.

I was also mourning the loss of what could have been with Miles. I'd played the scene over and over in my mind, trying to figure out what had changed. I'd mentioned to Jordan I would leave Monday, and Miles immediately distanced himself. What was his story, and did it matter to me if I was leaving? He was a comfort, a rock to my crumbling foundation, and my core was hurting. He understood me in a keen way, and had an uncanny ability to heal me.

He was everywhere in my dreams during the night, and I woke perplexed, lonely, and somehow rejected. I texted and invited him to join us for dinner with Brandan and Jordan, Jack and Callie, but the real reason was because I needed to see him again. I told him I was sure Nana would also be here for part of the time. He didn't respond, and the self-pity sank deeper into my psyche. When in the hell had I gotten to be such a fretful coward? I was taking myself way too seriously, and was starting to sound like the self-centered losers I was used to dating. This was the life I'd chosen. I needed to learn how best to deal with it.

Rather proud of the meal and dessert I'd prepared, the table setting, and the freshness of the entire house, I got my packing done for the following morning. I took great care with my appearance as I got ready, and looked forward to having everyone here. I'd forgotten how much I loved to entertain. *Right, Jeni,*

entertaining in someone else's home with someone else's things – that makes you a great hostess.

"*Please* will you consider staying?" Jordan begged as she walked through the dining room. "The house is always magnificent, but never has it looked more stunning than it does at this moment. I can't believe it!" She hugged me again as Brandan headed to their private suite on the third floor, Willow Tree, with their suitcases.

"You look fantastic. Obviously mountain air agrees with you."

"It's been as relaxing as any time I've had in years. It's going to be culture shock leaving."

"Riley wants me to open an office for Whitman and Burke in Denver. We talked a lot about it. I would never want to work full time as a lawyer again, but the thought of overseeing it has some appeal. Maybe you could take an office in a potential building and we could work together. Doesn't that sound like fun?"

"Yeah, I'm overwhelmed to the point of exhaustion, and the thought of having an office in New York *and* Denver excites the hell out of me," I said with no small degree of sarcasm. "Sure, sweetheart, I'll give that a considerable amount of thought."

We giggled and hugged as we headed to the kitchen to get the last of the meal ready. "So tell me about Miles. Was it wonderful?"

"What does that mean? It was over before it began. He made it clear he wants nothing to do with me, and that was the end of it."

"I know better than that. I've seen his yearning looks. He talks about you often to Brandan. What happened?"

"Nothing. He's not looking for a one-night stand, and apparently he's not looking for a long-distance relationship either. He made no bones about the fact that the beginning was also the end." I took food out of the refrigerator and set it on the counter.

"So I'm gonna suck it up and move on, and become celibate, and possibly join a convent if nothing else presents itself in the near future."

"If I heard correctly, you're thinking of joining a convent? Now that would truly be a shame," Miles said with a silly grin and a wink as he stepped through the back door with Nana on his arm. My heart rate and breathing started doing double time when I saw him, and I was determined we would enjoy this final evening together. He situated Nana on a stool at the counter and handed Jordan a bouquet of flowers.

"Welcome home, beautiful. These are for the dining room. I couldn't figure out which of you three gorgeous creatures to celebrate, so I decided to celebrate all of you."

"That's very nice of you," Brandan said, coming across the room to give Miles a warm greeting. "It's a good thing I trust you so much, bringing my wife flowers."

"He brought them for me, young man," Nana piped in. "He's my beau, so he's no threat to your wife."

We all laughed and worked companionably in the kitchen, sharing wine and hearing stories of Wiley Riley and what a cantankerous patient he'd been. Anxious to be released, he offered money to anyone who would listen if they would just help him escape. He also charmed the nurses into spending more time with him than they should have. He hadn't made it to his position without having a certain kind of dynamic charisma. My heart hammered every time I caught a glance of Miles, and I wondered if his pulse raced like mine when we accidentally touched. My skin tingled, and I'm sure my cheeks were flushed.

By the time Jack and Callie showed up, everything was ready for my farewell dinner. "What's on the menu?" Jack asked. "It smells delicious."

"Thanks! I had fun putting it together. We've got Stuffed Cornish Game Hens with Garlic and Rosemary, Risotto with Sun-Dried Tomatoes and Mozzarella, Prosciutto Wrapped Asparagus, and for dessert we've got White Chocolate Raspberry Cheesecake with White Chocolate Brandy Sauce."

Laughter and loud talk swirled as everyone took a seat and passed dishes. I had a high chair set up for Charlotte Rose, and she was thrilled to be part of the confusion. Enveloped in a cloak of friendship, I basked in the moments of joy we were sharing like a cat in the sharp sunlight of morning. Excusing myself through the swinging door to the kitchen to refill some of the now-empty dishes, I felt his presence before I heard him.

"Can I help with that?" he asked softly from the doorway.

My heart contracted. I turned away so he couldn't see my cheeks flame with hurt and rejection.

"No, I got it, thanks. I'm entirely capable on my own."

"Listen, Jeni, I don't want you to leave without explaining."

Trying to sound nonchalant, and masking that I was on the verge of tears from his gentle words, I said, "It's absolutely all right. I understand."

"You don't understand anything," he said, coming up behind me without touching. "We both know what there is between us, that will never be a question. But I can't do thousands of miles, and you can't stay. There aren't options for us. I refuse to do part time, so it is what it is."

"You're so right, I'm outta here and won't be back soon."

"I'm well aware. You've mentioned it more than once," he said almost harshly.

"I get it." I turned with a fake smile, refusing to let him see what this was doing to me, biting the inside of my cheek to keep the tears at bay.

"Jeni, I'm sorry." His tone turned tender. "I couldn't let you leave believing it hadn't meant something to me, too."

"Don't kid yourself, Miles. It was, in fact, a one-night stand. Nothing more, nothing less. You'll get over it." *Good grief, was that really necessary?* I asked myself as I picked up the dishes to head to the dining room.

"Stop it. You're not fooling me with your tough-guy routine, and you can't convince me you weren't as affected as I was. There wasn't a day after I met you that I didn't think about you. When your mother died, I thought about flying out to comfort you and drive back with you because I knew the pain of it. When I found out you were coming, I could hardly wait to see you. But I can't do this. I can't have you come back every now and then. It's not possible to sustain it in my life. I wanted you to know it has nothing to do with you, the person you are."

Still standing with dishes in my hands, my back to him, listening to his words, hating to be vulnerable and not knowing how to respond, I went back to the noise and din of the dining room. Later I would process what he'd said.

The first day back at work was surreal. Like a place out of time, it was as though they were speaking to someone else as everyone greeted me with enthusiasm and told me how glad they were I was finally back. Crandon's was on the schedule for a face-to-face meeting tomorrow, and we had a lot of work to do to be prepared to show them the campaign we'd been working on the past month. I was pleased and impressed with it, but it needed polishing before sending it to production for the final video draft before tomorrow.

Hannah was wonderfully creative and an asset I couldn't do without, but she carried childishness with her that sometimes interfered with her work, and I was ready for her to grow up.

"You can't keep pouting when things don't go your way, Hannah," I said, probably not as sympathetically as I could have while she paced in front of my desk.

"But you should have heard what Adam said about my tagline. It was downright insulting."

"Listen to me. We come up with fantastic campaigns by sharing ideas. While they might not have used your idea word for word, it was still the launching point for the final ad they came up with. This is a team effort unless it's your project, and it was the collective creative genius that made this what it became. I think we have a winner here, and you're the one that started the ideas flowing. You need to take pride in that and grow thicker skin."

"You really think it was a good idea?" she asked in her childlike manner. Dealing with creative personalities was a challenge unto itself, but I didn't have time for her nonsense.

"It was brilliant, but you need to learn how to play well with others or we're going to have to have a serious come-to-Jesus meeting. Consider this a warning. I'm tired of having to run interference because someone hurt your feelings. You're almost thirty, it's time to grow up."

I leaned against the edge of my desk as she sat in a chair looking like a beaten puppy. "You have stellar talent. You're a creative masterpiece in the making, and that makes you a little vulnerable and whacky. I understand completely. But if you want to succeed, if you want to reach your potential, you need to let things roll off your back. Take *their* ideas and let them fuel your creativity. Unless you want to work solo, you need to figure it out."

"Thank you," she said forlornly. "I'll try."

"Great. We have a huge day tomorrow, so take a few minutes, pull yourself together, and then let's buckle down. This is what we've all been working for. Let's show 'em what we're made of."

She hugged me as she left the room. "I'm so glad to have you back. You're the oil that keeps the gears running smoothly around here," she said before she closed the door behind her. A few months ago, that statement would have made my heart sing. Now I wondered why I just didn't care.

Lost in design elements for tomorrow's presentation, my heart turned over as the phone rang and I saw it was Miles.

"To what do I owe the pleasure?" I asked, shooting for nonchalance.

"I was thinking of you, and thought you'd appreciate a funny story about Nana. Got a minute?"

"Sure," I said, heart accelerating at the sound of his voice.

"I had business in town earlier today and stopped by the cottage to check on her, see how she was."

"That was nice of you."

"She was concerned about something," he continued. "Miriam went to the kitchen and Nana called me over furtively. Looking around to make sure no one else was there, she took my arm and shook her head several times. 'Do you hear that?'

"My mind is racing, naturally, trying to figure out where the conversation is heading, but I didn't really have a clue, so I whispered to her, 'What am I supposed to be hearing?'"

"'Well, the rocks, of course.'"

"So I'm still whispering and get closer and say, 'You have rocks in your head?'"

"'Listen!' she yelled at me and kept shaking her head."

"'Oh, now I hear them,' I agreed. 'Where do you suppose they came from?'"

"'I think Henry left them for me, but I don't want them any more. Will you take them when you leave?'"

"'Yes, I'll be glad to take them and get rid of them.'"

"'Don't get rid of them! Henry wanted me to have them. I just don't want them in my head any more.'"

"Oh, Miles, that's very funny and very sad at the same time."

"That's what I thought. She seemed agitated today, and I wanted so much to figure out a way to give her comfort."

"The familiarity of having you there has to be a comfort, and I can't thank you enough."

"You know it's no problem, I just wish I could help her. As I was leaving, Nana got a puzzled look on her face and said, 'You know that disease where you forget things?'"

"'You mean Alzheimer's?' I asked her."

"'Yes, yes, that's it. I think I have that,' she said very matter-of-factly."

"What's so tragic about all of this is how vital she used to be. She was brilliant, funny, compassionate, always there if anyone needed anything. My friends loved coming to our house because she was so much fun."

"You lived with her?"

Resting my feet on the desk, I watched the sunlight play through the wide expanse of window on my well-worn Ferragamo pumps. Maybe a new pair of shoes would make me feel better.

"Yeah, we lived in the house in Brooklyn." My mind could see the trees with red leaves in the front yard, the lawn that was always well manicured, and the flower pots of roses that seemed to always be in bloom.

"My mom told me Nana had a green thumb, and I remember sitting at the dining table, looking at her hands often but never being able to see the thumb that was supposed to be green. My dad died in a freak accident at work when I was six, and his company gave my mom a huge settlement – enough to pay off the house and let her live comfortably without having to work. When Grandpa Henry died two years later,

Nana was so lonely she came to live with us. It's all I ever knew. She was so young, and she and my mom got along well and spoiled me rotten. I was blessed."

"Sounds like it."

"Thanks, Miles," I said quietly. "You're a hell of a guy."

"See ya around, Jeni. Take care of yourself."

I sat for a few minutes, lost in the 'what ifs,' then got back to work. No sense dreaming about something I couldn't have.

CHAPTER ELEVEN

Crandon's was delighted with the campaign, and we were on our way to making something of our upstart young agency. There were a few changes we needed to make before it went into full-blown production, but it wasn't anything the staff couldn't handle without me, and I wouldn't be too far away. It was Wednesday afternoon and I was taking the rest of the week off, ready to face the house in Brooklyn. I wasn't sure what I'd find, but Callie's advice had been solid. Now wasn't the time to go through everything, it was just the time to sort what I wanted to keep, give away, and throw away. I had the system ready and would get as much done as I could. Mama was well organized, so I was hoping it wouldn't take more than the four or five days I'd allotted. It was going to be emotionally draining and I wanted it to be over, so I'd start first thing in the morning. As much as I was dreading it, I had to have it behind me to start my next chapter of life, whatever that turned out to be. The Salvation Army would be there Monday to pick up the donations, so I had a lot to do in the meantime.

Leaving the office early that afternoon, I thought of Jordan's kitchen as I passed The Strand Bookstore on my way to the subway. I wasn't in a hurry, so I popped in to find her something unique, maybe something with old recipes in it to use in her Victorian Bed and Breakfast. Finding just what I was looking for, I was lighter of spirit as I stopped to mail it, then slipped into a nearby bodega to grab a bite to eat.

ABBA was playing from the overhead speakers. Mom and I would dance from room to room when I was younger, cleaning to their music because she said it made the work go faster. I knew most of their songs by heart, and the words looped in my brain as I remembered the familiar refrain:

One of us is crying, one of us is lying
In her lonely bed, staring at the ceiling,
Wishing she was somewhere else instead.
One of us is lonely, one of us is only

Waiting for a call. Sorry for herself,

Feeling stupid, feeling small,

Wishing she had never left at all.

Hours later, lying in my bed, the words continued to circle in my head.

On rapid wings, the first two days in Brooklyn flew by. Nothing to stop me in my tracks, nothing more than the pang of sadness being in the house that still mourned the loss of its owners. I'd always appreciated my mother's sense of order, but I was now relieved and impressed with how little there was in the way of clutter. Since it was the largest room and easily accessible to the rest of the house, I started with the living room. I packed and cleaned so I could use it as the central location for future distribution.

With an eye toward putting the house on the market in the next week, I left a sparse amount of furniture for showings and moved the rest to one side in the main room so it could be taken out easily. Excess furniture from the three bedrooms was also moved there, and the bathrooms took little time to empty and clean.

The hardest part had been drawers and closets, the smell on her clothes causing immeasurable heartache. I went through every pocket to make sure nothing of value was left before I packed them away to donate. I pictured her in them, causing aching, wistful tears to softly fall as I remembered her generosity, the times we'd been together when she'd worn them, how much she loved me, and how much I was going to miss her strength in my life. She'd been selfless, and my hollow sobs were barely heard in the silence.

With an ebb and flow of thoughts, I had time to reflect in the stillness of memories. I had no tangible recollections of my father, only a sense of being well-loved, and what I'd seen in pictures. Sometimes there would be a fleeting smell of something in the house that would bring an elusive memory, but like the wind, I could never quite capture it before it was gone. Why had I always been attracted to men who thought they were the center of the known universe when the only influence in my life had been a spirit of giving?

Mama and I sat in her kitchen on more than one occasion as she tried to help me understand that I deserved so much more than what I'd been settling for.

Part of me always thought it was because it was easy — easy to get into, easy to get out of, no commitments. It never made sense to me because I wasn't lacking in self-esteem, but I'd had a taste of something better, of what a truly good man looked like, and the bitter aftertaste of men who were takers now seared my tongue. I didn't want 'easy' any more.

Knowing they'd take longer than the other rooms, I left the kitchen and family room for the last two days. Those were the rooms where they'd lived their daily lives. I'd been dreading it. Saturday morning found me moving furniture to the living room, packing lamps and magazines, going through desk drawers. There was a degree of intrigue as I opened the large bottom drawer crammed with papers. I crossed my legs and sat on the floor, setting everything in front of me to see what she'd found worthy to keep. It was a reflection of my entire life — report cards, kindergarten pictures, diplomas, awards, school pictures, letters I'd written. I knew I couldn't take the time to go through all of them now, so I placed it all in a box I would take to my co-op to go through when there was no deadline looming. I didn't even try to stop the tears.

The opposing drawer was just as crammed. The top picture was one I'd drawn when I was six. A picture of stick people, a small person had arms extended to the taller woman with a caption that read "Mommy." There was an angel at the top with childish handwriting, "Dont go see dady. Id miss yu."

The floodgates opened, remembering her unconditional love for me. I was desperately alone and craved human contact. Jordan was always there for me, always brave, always practical and loving. I dialed Miles' number.

"Hey, what's up?" he said as he answered the phone.

I just kept crying, inconsolable, wondering why I'd bothered him.

"Jeni, what's the matter, honey? What happened? Talk to me. Are you all right?"

"Uh huh," I managed to get out. "I'm sorry, Miles. I needed someone who'd understand, and you were the only one I could think of."

"What's going on? Take your time."

"I've been dealing well with it. Not crying much, missing her but not falling apart." I blew my nose. "Sorry."

"Go on."

"Then I opened this drawer and there were all these things she'd saved from my entire lifetime. My first lock of hair, my baby bracelet from the hospital, a birthday card I'd given my dad when I was five. A lifetime of someone who loved me so much and thought these things were special enough to keep when she didn't keep anything else that wasn't absolutely necessary. I'm sorry, I shouldn't have called. I'll be fine."

"Don't you dare hang up. Start pacing, it'll help you think things out."

"How do you know that?"

"I've watched you do it enough times, and I've seen how it helps your brain click in."

"You're amazing," I said, somewhat in awe.

"Listen. More than anyone, I do understand what you're going through. I wasn't so lucky that my mom was as orderly as yours. It took me weeks to go through everything."

As I continued to weep, he said, "This is part of grieving. Don't try to stop it, let it out while you can. You'll be wrung out, but tomorrow you'll be a step ahead. Today won't be the only time it happens. It may happen five times, it may be a dozen. But here's an idea that liberated me. It doesn't all have to come in a nice little package of time. You'll mourn her death for the rest of your life."

"I knew it was you I was supposed to call," I said, thankful for his compassionate ear. "It's somehow soothing to understand that. You're right, I don't ever want to get to a point that I don't miss her. But right now I feel such regret. I loved her so much, but I never had enough time for her. There was always something else that needed to be done, work that needed to be completed, one more letter that needed to be written. And when I was with her, I was distracted with business, with clients, with things that prevented me from being in the moment with her. How do you forgive yourself?"

"If you'd been there holding her hand everyday, you would still blame yourself about something. Trust me. I was by mom's side for months, taking care of her, talking to her, helping her as much as I could to face what we all knew was around the corner. I couldn't have done more for her, but when she passed, I thought of all the things I wish I'd said, all the things I wish I'd taken care of before she got sick."

"Oh, Miles, I'm sorry."

"They knew how much we loved them, Jeni. Don't beat yourself up over it. Grieve her loss, of course, but forgive yourself. It will only cloud and delay your healing. You can't ever doubt how much she loved you and wanted you to be happy. Besides, it would break her heart to know you were grieving over yourself and not her," he said with a smile in his voice.

"Thanks for that reality check. Having had so much time here, I think the biggest sorrow of all is how much I didn't realize how bad Nana was. I can't conceive of what it was like to take care of her without any help, and she didn't even have me. I came for dinner once or twice a week if I could spare the time, but I only put more of a burden on her. I didn't help with what was important, and I feel somehow partly responsible for her death."

"Stop it, *now*. Listen, even if . . ." The doorbell rang.

"Would you hold on a minute and let me see who's at the door?" I asked, climbing over boxes.

"I'm not going anywhere."

There was not a human being I cared to see right now, and the man standing on the doorstep topped the list.

"You're looking a bit disheveled. Mind if I come in?"

"Yes, I do mind. What do you want, Jared?"

"Just came by to see my old girl," he said, pushing into the living room as though I hadn't spoken, looking around at the mess. "Aren't you glad to see me? It's been a while."

"I'm busy right now," I said, eyes narrowing.

"Couldn't figure out yesterday when I called your office why you'd want to be out here."

"I'm getting the house ready to put on the market. Why would you call, and what brought you so far out of your way?" I asked with a noticeable degree of irritation.

"I wanted to see you, of course," he said, examining items, then setting them down as though they'd not been worth his effort.

"Did you hear my mother died?" I asked.

"Yeah, too bad. Did you hear I got a promotion?" He headed into the kitchen and opened a cabinet. "How much do you suppose you can get for this place?" he asked as he filled a glass with water.

What in God's name did I ever find attractive about him? There was nothing handsome about his chiseled features once you knew his dark soul behind it. Now I couldn't imagine suffering through a dinner with this heartless, unfaithful bastard, much less having wasted precious months of my life on him, having found out the hard way he didn't believe in monogamy. What a loser. Maybe it was me who needed therapy.

"I'm sure you weren't just driving by, and it's obvious you didn't come to offer your condolences, so what do you need?"

"You used to love having me around," he said, coming closer. "We had some good times together." He raised his hand to touch my cheek.

"Don't you dare touch me. I want you to leave . . . *now*."

"I need you, Jeni. No one else has the magic you do, and there wasn't anyone else I could ask."

"Ask what?" I couldn't think of what he could possibly be talking about.

"They saw some of your ads at work. I told them I'd done them, part of why I got the promotion. So I have this project due Tuesday," he said, unrolling papers he held in his hand.

"*Excuse* me?" I said, not believing what I was hearing.

"Come on, it's important. You and I used to work well together, remember?"

"You mean you sat around while I did your work for you? Is *that* how we worked well together?" I asked sarcastically.

"That's not fair. We sparked great ideas off each other. Remember the Wyseman campaign?"

"Are you for real? I came up with the idea, the slogan, the video theme, and you changed one word. Get out, Jared. You bore me." I rubbed my temples to ward off the impending headache.

His voice was a little sterner when he said, "Maybe I didn't explain well enough. They're expecting the same caliber work that got me the job in the first place. I thought I could do it, but you come up with ideas like that," he said, snapping his fingers. "I've been working on it for days and can't even figure out how to make it sound like I'd want to use their product. It won't take you any time at all."

"That's for sure. It's not even gonna take one more minute of my time," I said, holding the door open. "If we ever see each other in passing, pretend like we've never met. I promise I'm not going to acknowledge you."

"Is it money you want? I'll pay you."

Somewhere in my head I wondered if I looked like a fish with my mouth agape. "Get out of here, Jared," I said, controlling my rising anger, patience wearing thin.

He had stepped to the front porch and was still talking when I slammed the door as hard as I could, then locked and chained it. It took about five seconds, but my anger and frustration were so great I let out a deep primal scream that could only be described as a roar.

"*Jeni! Jeni! Are you all right?*"

I had completely forgotten Miles was on the phone. Shit, he'd heard the entire conversation. I was mortified.

"Is it too much to hope you put the phone down and did some chores while that was going on?" I said, somewhat sheepishly.

"Do you have any idea how difficult that was to be almost two thousand miles away and not have any way to help if that'd turned ugly? I don't even have your address there to call 911 if I'd had to. Why did you yell?"

Now I *was* embarrassed. "Frustration, stupidity, incredulous I ever dated him, you know, self-esteem issues. And you heard it all."

"You were terrific. I was proud of you, but then I heard you scream. I wasn't sure if he'd come back or not."

"You wouldn't be proud of me if you knew I wasted months of my life on that jerk. I'm humiliated."

"Wanna talk about it?"

"Why would I even think of telling you how stupid I am?"

CHAPTER TWELVE

"Because I can see you biting the inside of your cheek in your confusion. Because you're going through a lot and you need all the pieces to fit, and guys like Jared are one of the pieces that need to be worked out. I bet your mom didn't like him."

"Couldn't stand him. Couldn't even be civil to him for me. God, don't remind me. She thought I'd taken leave of my senses. She was right. I wish I could tell her how right she was."

"She knows, don't worry. And you broke it off before she died, so *some* of your senses came back," he teased.

"I thought he was a pain in the neck before, but now I have an even lower opinion of him. What a fool I was."

His rumbling laughter eased my ache a little. "You convince yourself you're happy," I said, "but the truth of the matter is things are swirling around you and you don't slow down enough to use your brain, it's just convenient. We traveled in the same circles, it was easy, and I wasn't even conscious of the man beneath the mask. It was my mom who made me see something was wrong with him, glaringly wrong."

"Trust me, when you're too close to the situation, sometimes it's difficult to see what's under your nose, and what everyone else has seen all along."

"I know. And as you try to pick up the pieces of your soul you've allowed them to shred, they pull you back in and convince you your doubts about them are all wrong."

"I'm sorry, Jeni."

"Don't be sorry. It was my own stupidity. And what I've never been able to figure out is how, when they decide to be nice and weasel their way back in, you convince yourself it was *you* who did something wrong, and wonder how you could have been so wrong and misunderstood their intentions."

"Yep. You lose the argument with yourself that it's over and you need to break the ties."

"Sounds like you've had experience with toxic affairs in the past," I hinted, hoping he'd open up.

"In a different way than you, but I'm all too familiar with what happens when you finally find the power to leave, and they hold on just enough to give you hope so you never really let go of them – until you do."

"Wanna talk about it?" I asked, digging.

"Nope, but thanks for the offer. I really gotta go. Glad you're feeling better. I'm writing down funny Nana stories. I'll share them sometime."

"Oh! I'd love that!"

"Take care of yourself. It might not seem like it now, but there are rainbows on the other side of the clouds."

"I appreciate you. Thanks for answering your phone."

I felt stronger. The painful tears, the confrontation, the understanding – I was able to finish packing boxes and move the family room furniture I'd be giving away. It had been a heartbreaking but productive day, and Miles was right – there were rainbows waiting for me.

Miles. It was the best conversation we'd had since I left. Visions of him were with me as I finished up the last of the family room. I was restless. There wasn't anyone here I cared to see, but I didn't want to be alone. It was two hours earlier in Colorado, so I called Jordan.

"Am I interrupting something?" I asked, hearing Brandan in the background.

"No, he's just telling Miles goodbye."

"Miles?"

"Yeah, he comes over every day, rain or shine, weekday, weekend, work day, everyday, to check on Nana. He's wonderfully devoted to her, even when she doesn't know who he is, or when she thinks he's Henry."

"God, Jordan, he's something, isn't he?"

"He is, indeed. Something sad happened the other day, made me really appreciate him. We were standing in the kitchen, Miles, Nana, Brandan, and I, when Nana lifts up her shirt and asks Miles if he wants to touch her boobs."

"*What? That's so awful!*"

"She called him Henry, but he put his body between us so no one could see her, and tenderly pulled her shirt down. He put his arm around her and told her she was too tired, and walked her back to the cottage."

"All of this makes me so miserable," I said.

"I know, honey, but it's working for now. It's the way it is for the time being, but she's got a lot of support around her, and we all love her like she was our own. We're taking good care of her."

"I don't want to cry any more, Jord, but I can't seem to stop. I'll be done with the house tomorrow, and Callie gave me a referral for a Realtor. She's coming out on Tuesday, and we can, hopefully, get it sold in a hurry. I'm so adrift, and seem to have lost my direction. Business is great but I don't even care. What's the matter with me?"

"Stop beating yourself up. Give it time. Seriously, all of this has been a complete shock. You found your healthy mother dead, then you drove Nana across country, Riley had a heart attack, you took over for me, you fell in love, then left a sensational guy, you have to -"

"Wait! Hold on! What do you mean I 'fell in love'?"

"Hey, it's me. I know you, sometimes better than you know yourself. Whether you acknowledge the truth or not, it doesn't negate that it's a fact. If you ask me, you fell in love with each other the day you met, you just didn't have a clue what hit you because you didn't have anything to base it on. I recognize it, and I'm telling you, darlin', it's love."

"It can't possibly be. He made it clear we have no future. He doesn't want me as a fixture in his life. There are too many risks in trying to change that."

"In the decades I've known you, I've never known you to back down from a challenge."

"My life is here, his life is there. Done, finished, over. Period. What are you trying to accomplish with this line of reasoning, counselor?"

"Brandan won't tell me Miles' story, but he did say Miles carries his own baggage, and it's pretty heavy. He said you're not the only history Miles has left behind. Brandan says it would take someone incredibly dedicated to break through the walls he's put up. You seem to have a strong enough connection."

"And a lot of holes in the chain. Thanks for thinking of me, but that'll have to be someone else's job."

"Chicken."

"Bitch."

The mood was lightened with our mirth. "Besides, he's the nicest person I've known in my life. What would I do with him?"

"I'm sure you'd think of something."

"Thanks for making me feel better. Thanks for letting me know my grandmother is trying to get my love interest to feel her up. It just gets better and better."

"I'm sorry about Nana," she said sympathetically. "Miles studies the disease all the time to see if there's anything new they can use to try to stop the progression of it. They're making great strides with some new medicines."

"Why hasn't he told me?"

"How should I know? He works all day, has his own life, studies her disease, visits her, and never loses his cool. You're right, it should be someone else's job to break through those walls he's put up."

"You really *are* a bitch, aren't you?"

"Just sayin'. Anyway, gotta go, I got a hot man waitin' for me. Love you. Glad you're almost done. Get some sleep. It's gonna be stressful."

"Thanks for everything, sweetheart. I'll never be able to repay you. Give that gorgeous hunk a huge kiss for me."

"Will do. Night."

Packing the kitchen the next day, I could think of little else besides Miles. What *was* his story? What had someone done to him that could make him so opposed to involvement? Why was he spending so much time studying Nana's disease? His face intruded on the mundane. Rather than becoming maudlin getting rid of things my mother had owned, I kept thinking about this different type of loss, one I had chosen, and one I couldn't seem to find a way out of. My mother would have loved him, and would be so glad I was finally interested in a kind man.

Finished with the packing and arranging of furniture, I was ready for them to take the donations tomorrow, then I'd clean and be ready for the Realtor on Tuesday. I wondered what Miles was doing right now. Should I call him and ask about Nana? Should I truly walk away and let him go? Was Jordan right? Had it been love at first sight? I was making myself miserable with this line of thinking. There was no future. It would be difficult to go back and see Nana if it meant I'd also have to see him. My heart yearned for him, but he'd made his decision and I had never been good at relationships. On the other hand, it was easy to be a failure when only one of you was involved.

Jordan said she thought Miles had fallen in love that day, too. What did I mean, "too"? Was I in love with Miles? It didn't make any difference, the obstacles were great, and I was too tired to think any more. I hated crying. It wore me out.

The sun filtering through the curtains woke me eight hours later. Good grief! I *must* have been exhausted. The donation center would be here in less than an hour and I wasn't even dressed. I was thankful for a good night's sleep. I felt rested, and the light of day put a new perspective on my reflections. My mom and I had been close, and this was the end of decades of her life. It took everything in me to watch them haul it out.

As the truck pulled away, I couldn't help but wonder how the body has the ability to produce so many tears. With everything removed, there was little left to clean. The house was so neat there wasn't much more to do than dust and rinse the sinks and tubs. I called the Realtor to see if she could come over today and not wait until tomorrow, to which she agreed. The sooner we started, the sooner we'd be finished. It had been a long week and I wanted to be done.

I'm not sure how it happened, but I looked at the phone in my hand and it was dialing Miles' number.

"Hello?"

"Hi."

"Yes?"

"It's Jeni."

"Like I didn't know. What do you need?"

"It's done. Almost all the furniture is gone, the cleaning is finished, most of her personal possessions have been donated, the Realtor will be here soon. I was feeling lost and looking for a friendly voice. I obviously got a wrong number."

There was a pause. "I'm sorry. I know how tough it is." His voice gentled. "But look at what you accomplished this week. Not many people could've done what you did in so short a time. It was a major accomplishment."

A sob caught in my throat. "Don't be nice to me, it makes me cry." I knew I sounded foolish. Is this what sabotaging a relationship looks like?

"So make up your mind. You can't have it both ways. Which way do you want me, hard or soft?"

"What?"

"You didn't like the hard jerk who answered the phone, but then you tell me it makes you cry when I'm soft and sympathetic. So which way do you want me?" he teased.

"Thank you, Miles. You're exactly what I needed. Gotta go, the Realtor's at the door."

"Good luck."

"Miles?"

"Yes, Jeni."

"I'll take it hard any day."

I heard his laughter as he hung up.

I'd been back to work for almost three weeks. We received two offers on the property the week it was listed, and the process was proceeding faster than I could have imagined. I went to the house often, knowing when the sale was final, this chapter of my life would be over, no turning back. Even understanding her essence would always be with me, there was something poignant about being in this place where I'd spent so many happy years, where my mother's presence was in every corner and hallway, and where the memory of my joyful grandmother still resided. This, by far, was going to be the highest hurdle.

One night I laid on her bed weeping. She had spent so much time here, I wanted to feel her. Her spirit left her body from this spot, and I felt close to her. "I miss you so much, Mama. I love you."

"Love you, Jeni Marie," I heard faintly.

It was a name she'd called me for as long as I could remember. Was I losing my mind? "Mama?"

No sound, no echo, total silence. "Are you here, Mama?"

Nothing. Goose bumps covering my arms, I backed out of the room and decided I was tired and had been here long enough. When I got to my co-op, I kept remembering the voice that had used my mother's pet name for me. I called Miles.

"Please tell me I'm not crazy," I said as he answered the phone.

"It's not in my nature to lie, Jeni."

"You can always make me laugh. Listen, something strange happened to me tonight." I told him the story. There was silence on the other end. "Are you still there?"

"Yes, I'm here."

"*Now* do you think I'm crazy? What do you supposed it was?"

"I think there are things we'll never understand."

"What are you saying? And which one of us do you think is crazy?" I asked, trying to inject some humor.

"*You* asked *me.* Do you want me to tell you what I think, or do you want me to give you platitudes?"

"I want your honest opinion, Miles. I heard her clear as day. It was faint, but no one else has ever called me that. I figured I just wanted her to be there so much I made it up."

"You'll probably think I'm certifiable when I tell you this, but I think it was your mom."

"You're not serious!"

"You asked, and that's honestly what I think. Listen, I can't explain it, and we'll never know the answers in this lifetime, but I had something similar happen to me about two months after my mom passed. Are you open to hearing this?"

"Of course I am. Go on."

"It was early morning and I was shaving. I saw something move behind me in the mirror. I focused on it, and it was my mother, only she was young and healthy. Thinking I must be tired, I got closer to the mirror to see her better. She blew me a kiss and had a loving, peaceful smile.

"I turned quickly to catch a glimpse of what could be causing such a reflection, but nothing was there. No wind blew, nothing that could've given a hint of what I'd seen. For weeks I believed I'd hallucinated her because she'd been in pain for so long and I wanted desperately for her to be healthy. Then one night when I was asleep, the same vision appeared, only this time she told me she loved me. When I tried to reach for her, she was gone as quickly as she'd appeared.

"From that day, I had a new understanding. I've never told anyone that story until just now, and I'll deny it if you ever repeat it," he laughed, "but in my heart I've always thought she'd found a way to let me release her, and I did. She was healthy and young and beautiful again, and I knew she was free."

Still having no idea where all these tears came from, I sat silently, visualizing what he'd seen, believing the story he'd told me, and knowing true joy at the possibility of what I'd heard.

"Sorry you called?" he asked.

"No, you have a unique ability to bring me comfort. My heart can understand what I heard, even if my brain can't." No longer hampered by the undeniable fact, I said, "If I hadn't been in love with you before, I'd pretty well guarantee I am now." Did I really let those words pass my lips?

It was his turn to be silent. After a painfully long time, he said softly, "Don't do this to us, Jeni." Another long pause, he said, "Take care of yourself." The phone went dead.

CHAPTER THIRTEEN

Days turned to weeks. The house in Brooklyn sold, and with it brought a finality to that portion of my life. "You can never go home again" was a phrase I thought of often. My creative juices were flowing, and we couldn't have handled more business. I was busy, but happiness was missing from my life.

I spoke with Jordan daily and got a regular update from the nurses. They were going to bring on a third nurse, and Miles had put himself in charge of the screening process. By the world's standards, I had arrived. I had everything I'd set out to achieve, but my life felt empty.

There were always people around me, so why was I lonely? I socialized with friends, business acquaintances, coworkers, and at the end of the day, I went home alone because that's the way I wanted it. There were offers, but my time with Miles spoiled me for other men. After what we'd shared, how could I think of being with someone else? I didn't want an entanglement, and I didn't want to waste my time with someone with whom I couldn't have an intimate connection outside of the bedroom as well. I just wasn't interested.

Miles called every now and then to share stories about Nana and to check on me. She seemed to be holding her own, and for right now, didn't seem to be sliding too quickly down the slippery slope. It would happen in time, but the new medicines they were giving her seemed to be slowing the progression. Our conversations were never personal, and if I tried to make them so, he ended them abruptly.

In what little free time I had, I became introspective. The irreverent, devil-may-care woman of last year was replaced with someone I was coming to respect. In the alone time I had with myself, I considered the mistakes I'd made in the past, not only in business, but in failed personal relationships. I often thought of my mother, and the things I would've changed if given an opportunity. I stopped beating myself up over what I hadn't done, and made peace knowing I would never have the opportunity to change those things. As much as I was able during her lifetime, she knew I loved her. There was never a question she loved me.

What I could never seem to escape was my current reality. I had a business, responsibilities, an incredible support team, but I didn't have family. Nana was getting older in a hurry, had dementia, and I had hired the best staff possible to meet her needs. But others were taking care of her, were loving her, and she'd lost everyone she'd ever known. I'd worked hard the last few months to let go of remorse caused by circumstances I had no control over, but Nana's situation wouldn't loosen its grip on my heart. Dozens of times I anticipated the phone call that would come one day to tell me she'd died, and I tried to imagine what I would've wanted to have done differently if given the opportunity beforehand, while she was still alive.

Leaning on the rail one afternoon, the smell of warm wind coming off the Hudson River, the ABBA song took up residence in my head again.

One of us is crying, one of us is lying
In her lonely bed, staring at the ceiling,
Wishing she was somewhere else instead.
One of us is lonely, one of us is only
Waiting for a call. Sorry for herself,

Feeling stupid, feeling small,
Wishing she had never left at all.

The answer was unexpectedly clear. I was young, healthy, and had a lifetime ahead of me. I wanted to be with Nana while there was still time. I could arrange my life to make that happen, and while her death might bring regrets, it would devastate me if I hadn't done everything possible while I still had the opportunity.

I was good at what I did, and current technology gave me an avenue to work no matter where I was. I didn't need a fancy office in Manhattan to do my design elements, and the rest of it could be worked out.

The next morning, I called everyone into the conference room to tell them of my decision. Met initially with opposition, they got somewhat excited when they understood I would still have an active role in not only the management of the company, but would certainly continue to be involved in ad campaigns. They were even more excited when we started talking about opening an office in either Denver or Boulder or both. Many meetings with accountants and attorneys took place over the next few weeks to make arrangements for the smooth transition of the running of the business. I hired a company to sublet my co-op, and Jordan and I were like schoolgirls at the prospect of living in close proximity again.

She finally agreed to allow me to pay rent for a room at Madeline Manor until I knew what I was doing, see how things worked out, and to give me time to get on my feet for this next piece of life's puzzle. I didn't know where it would fit when I got there, but I was at peace with my decision. And, truth be told, Miles was part of the equation and was worth fighting for. I didn't want to do this without him. What we had was enticing enough to work on, and I couldn't make anything happen from New York.

Jordan and I agreed we wouldn't mention it to Miles, so it was dazzlingly satisfying to see his face glow like the setting sun when he walked into the kitchen and saw me washing dishes. My world suddenly filled with color.

"Did I miss something?" he said, looking at me much as he had the first time we'd met in this same place.

"Me, maybe?" I teased, trying to catch my breath from the crazy things happening to my heart.

Jordan left the room without saying a word, and I was alone with a man who had taken up residence in my mind and consumed my thoughts.

"When did you get in?" he asked, not breaking eye contact.

"Last night. Nana actually recognized something about me, and immediately proceeded to relate to me as Janet. I was happy with that."

"How long you here for?" he asked, devouring me with his eyes.

"My plans are up in the air." We'd all agreed not to mention to anyone that I'd uprooted and was going to be a permanent fixture around here in the foreseeable future. I especially wanted to see if we could establish a bond without restrictions, break through his barriers because he wanted me, not because of where I lived. But for now it was enough to be in the same room with him, doing that outlandish thing we do, being aware of another human on a level I'd never known existed.

We could've stood there for one minute or five, I had no concept of time. What I *did* know is that I loved this man, and I wasn't going away without a fight. Holding his gaze, I walked over and stood in front of him, studying the face that was part of my heart. "Try as I might," I said, putting my hand on his chest, "I haven't been able to talk myself out of loving you. It's not my intention to make you uncomfortable, I just wanted to give you fair warning."

His arms wrapped around me, bringing me tight against his chest as his lips found mine. It was a searing kiss that reflected the hunger in both of us, and I knew I was home. I'd have to convince him of that, but all in due time.

"Welcome home," he said quietly, wiping an errant tear from my cheek.

"I was thinking the same thing."

He held on to me, my head resting comfortably on his shoulder. "What am I going to do with you?" he asked, holding my face, kissing me gently.

"Would you like me to suggest a few things?"

"I remember all too well."

"I've ached for you in places I didn't know I had."

"That's never been an issue for us," he said, pushing my hair behind my ear. It felt so right being with him. He let go of me and walked to the door. "I'll be back later."

"Wanna come for dinner?"

A smile played across his face, "Do *you*?" he asked, closing the door. My blood rushed when I realized what he'd said. I had a staggering sense of well being.

The clamor of dishes being passed, companionable laughter, and stories shared in voices loud enough to be heard over the din settled into the empty spaces in my heart. Each time Brandan reached for Jordan's hand, their eyes met briefly, speaking gently to each other, not using words. Miles leaned closer to Miriam, attentive and involved in whatever they were discussing. Every now and then he would look up and our eyes would meet. Without looking away, the caress of his glance was tangible on my cheek and in my spirit.

James Gabriel and Nana whispered, their words never heard above the noise. Occasionally one of them would raise their eyes, furtively looking around at the others assembled in this room that was the setting for many happy memories. James Gabriel was the only person who didn't seem to bring confusion to her about his role in her life. She always recognized Miles, but she was usually muddled about whether he was her son, grandson, boyfriend, or husband. Adaptable, he rolled with the punches in whatever capacity he'd been chosen to play that day.

Jack was a natural as a father. He carried Charlotte Rose in the crook of his arm, leaning against his chest, giving her a ringside seat to absorb the activity swirling around her. Hints of red highlights in her hair reflected from the soft glow of the Victorian chandelier that hung above the center of the magnificent mahogany table. Her contribution to the conversation came intermittently with adorable gurgles as she tested her vocal chords, "mamas" and "dadas" loud enough to be noticed, and occasionally stopping the banter as everyone broke into laughter. Jack was indulgent when I asked to hold her while everyone else ate.

Was anyone else aware of my total devotion and affection for this engaging child, my heart melting as she joyfully extended her arms for me to take over cushioned-chair duty? I would have to remember to apologize to Claire for not comprehending at the time her desire to stay home with her premature baby. Charlotte Rose was the first young child I'd spent time around, and now I understood the instincts that made people want to be parents. It may not be for everyone, but overwhelming longing rose in me as this cherub studied my face, first with her eyes, then her chubby fingers, and then her lips. Miles seemed to understand as our gazes held each other. I envied this.

CHAPTER FOURTEEN

The floorboards creaked faintly as Jordan and Brandan moved around on the third floor. The pleasant confusion of the evening gave way to soft night murmurs in front of the flickering flames of the fireplace in the parlor. The lights were out, and everyone had left but Miles, our voices low, a small space between us, discussing a breakthrough they were making with drug combinations to regulate chemicals that transmit messages between neurons.

"I've also been reading about natural remedies, especially coconut oil, that they say can help dementia patients maintain thinking and memory for longer. It seems to improve speech patterns, and they're finding it's even useful in reigning in behavioral problems."

When I didn't respond, he turned toward me, "You still awake?"

"Mm hmmm."

"Not finding this exciting at this time of night?" he laughed.

"Actually it is, but I was thinking of other things."

"Like what?"

"Us," I said, moving my gaze to meet his.

The sound of the flames could be heard in the stillness, casting a flickering glow against his beard-roughened chin. I savored the almost tangible rich, warm silence, and was cozy enough to let it continue. There was no need for a response, I'd said what I wanted to say. I had no intention of playing coy at this point. I knew what I wanted, and he was sitting inches away. It wasn't as though he weren't attracted to me, that had never been a concern. I was relaxed enough from the wine and the company to find it charming watching his face as he wrestled with his issues, but mostly I wanted to be with him.

"Emeralds," he said.

"Hmmmm?" I said only softly enough for him to hear.

"I think of emeralds when I see your eyes. Flashing, precious, transparent, reflective, tough but fragile."

His dark evening stubble was rough as I drew my sensitive fingertips over his cheek. He didn't break eye contact as he lowered his head for our lips to meet.

His tongue wet my waiting mouth, and I was in no hurry. This was the only place I wanted to be. "I should've left when everyone else did," he said, his breath warming my neck. "Only a fool would've believed I could resist you."

His words started a small flame that I knew could flare out of control with only a slight provocation. "I have no strength to fight this thing that's between us, but it doesn't change the outcome." His lips and tongue continued to caress the sensitive hollow of my neck, while his calloused fingers wove a path through my hair.

Leaning my head back against the palm of his hand, giving him full exposure to my neck, the words were breathless when I said, "What if I change the rules of engagement?"

His hesitation was slight as he lowered me to the soft cushions of the full-length couch, trembling firelight in the darkened room setting the tone for the gentleness between us. His gaze held me through the fan of his long, thick eyelashes. Half of his face now shadowed as he straddled me, slowly unbuttoning one button, then another of his well-worn, age-softened shirt that concealed the muscles of his chest and biceps. When he was finished, he lowered his hand to find the warmth at the apex of my thighs. I groaned with the shooting pleasure of the heightened nerve endings of my now-moist crotch, pressing into his palm as much as I could through my slacks and the confinement of his thighs around mine.

He ran a finger between my legs, teasing me, pressing against me, his breathing growing heavier with mine. He unbuttoned my pants, then slid the zipper down slowly with his thumb and forefinger, his little finger pressing into me in an insistent rhythm. I lifted my hips, but I was no match for his weight. There was nothing angelic about his shadowed smile as his focus shifted to the still-confined parts of our bodies that were touching, both of us knowing we wanted them flesh-to-flesh.

"It doesn't matter what I'm doing, you're there." His strained words were spoken so softly I wasn't sure I'd heard him. One of his legs straightened, causing a slight creak from the polished oak floor as he lifted his body off mine. He remained gentle as his trembling hands slowly slid my pants down my legs, legs that were straining to help remove them. He tenderly lifted my shirt over my head, dropping both soundlessly to the soft Victorian area rug.

When I purchased the elegant bra, I fantasized about how he might react to my breasts cupped in its sheer lace. What I couldn't have imagined was my body's response to the lust I saw flare in his eyes as his hands covered me, squeezing my aching mounds, catching my hardened nipples between this thumb and forefinger. My hand reached for him, wanting to free his swollen heat from the confines of his pants. As my hand found him, he stilled, allowing me to explore, his eyes closing, head falling back ever so slightly while I massaged him. The soft glow of the room would be forever imprinted in my mind as it played across his masculine features, intensifying the desire to touch him.

He stood and made eye contact as he teased his zipper down, his life force springing between us. He made a production of taking off first one pant leg, then the other as his jeans joined mine on the floor. He removed his shirt then gently lifted my hips with one arm as he slid it under me with his other. "Don't want to have to explain what happened to their couch," he smiled. His shirt acting as a shield beneath me, he lowered his head and flicked his tongue over my dripping warmth, lapping and licking my closed lips as he held my legs together. Wanting desperately to open myself to him, he said, "Not yet," and stood beside me.

He touched his engorged shaft with one hand while moving his other hand to cup his balls. After stroking himself a few times, revealing a head that was almost purple, I raised myself on an elbow to get closer. He leaned over and gently unhooked my bra, removing it as I reached for him. His tip glistened temptingly, and my tongue was desperate to taste his sweetness. Moving his hips, knees resting on the edge of the couch, he glided in and out of my wet mouth, at first just an inch or so, then thrusting further and further to have me take as much of him as I could. When his prodding hit the back of my throat, I reflexively pressed against him, bringing a cry of pleasure from his lips.

Footsteps could again be heard faintly from the third floor as we both stilled, waiting to make sure no footfall hit the stairs. My tongue circled his rim as we remained silent, and the play of light on his muscles as he strained not to move was an aphrodisiac. My fingers circled the base of his shaft as he again began moving in and out, and I yielded in pleasure as his fingers parted me and found their way into my throbbing wetness. Hips rising to meet him, he expertly pressed in just the right place, then slowed and gentled as I felt myself on the brink. "Not yet," he said again. "I want like hell for you to be on top, riding us both until we can't stand it."

He didn't have to ask twice. I rolled and stood as he took his shirt and laid it on the soft rug, then laid on top of it. He situated himself so my knees would be on the shirt. Marveling at my body's ability to accommodate his size, I knelt between his legs, taking him between both my hands, running his tip between my teeth and cheek. It drove him wild, and he pushed harder, filling my cheek and holding the thrust.

Moving up his body, I positioned my breast above his mouth. His tongue brushed roughly against my nipple as his hands pulled me tighter against his face, then took me into his mouth, sucking until the nerve endings were concentrated under his rhythmic tongue. His hands lowered to my hips, guiding me over his hardness. I sat up, rocking my wetness over his driving head, not taking him inside, but pressing to stimulate us both for the satisfaction to come. His hands pressed me harder against him as we glided over each other, nerve endings engorged in ecstasy. Lifting slightly above him, I reached behind to guide him to my eager lips, then took him fully, all at once.

My body spasmed around him as his hips lifted to fill me as I ground hard against him.

One hand guided the rhythm of my hips while his other found my swollen nub, teasing at first, then pressing harder to bring me the satisfaction we both craved. The flames in the fireplace couldn't match the heat between us as I rode his steel-hard shaft, not wanting to make noise but knowing that the clenching muscles that pulled at him as he pumped harder into me would release a hard climax that would be felt throughout my entire body. He grabbed my hair with his fist and pulled me toward him, watching me, our bodies now searching for release. I began to jerk violently and felt his hips convulse as he buried himself one last, hard, glorious time inside me, his hot lips covering mine to swallow the scream of satisfaction that couldn't help escape as I felt his warm ejaculation, pleasure tearing through me.

Collapsing on top of him, he caressed my back, causing my body to cool as he massaged the slight film of perspiration covering me. He touched me tenderly, holding me as he rolled us to the side, keeping me in his embrace, running his tongue soothingly over my lips as the last of my spasms subsided around him. Fire was mirrored in his eyes that looked like warmed brandy and became molten gold during passion. Was it the reflection of my love I saw, or did his eyes say what his words had not?

"What rules of engagement?" he asked.

Trying to catch up to the conversation, I remembered what I'd said before we began our electrifying interlude. "It's been my understanding that it wasn't *me* you didn't want to be involved with, that it was the distance between us that was the cause of your aloofness."

"That's a part of it," he said cautiously.

The lines of his face were etched permanently in my brain. Rarely was it not behind my eyelids when I closed them, and I wanted to make this happen, whatever the undeniable thing was between us. "What if there wasn't a distance?" I asked.

"What do you mean?"

"What if I didn't leave? What if I stayed?"

He didn't say anything, and that was okay. It had to have come out of left field, and I knew he was processing the possibility. "For one thing, I would never ask you to do that. You have a life in New York, a career in New York, and this is a backwater town where you'd shrivel after a while. No lights, no excitement, just a quiet life. It would hurt me to take that away from you."

"I've had more excitement in the last half hour than I've had since the last time I was here," I teased. "Not like I'm kicking up the high life. I work, I sleep, the next day I start all over again."

"It's not as easy as that," he said, his thumb stroking my cheek. "There are other things involved that we've never talked about because you being here was never a possibility."

"Listen, I can do my job anywhere. Jordan and Callie and I have even been talking about taking office space in one of Jack's buildings, either in Boulder or Denver or both. Almost everything I do is online, and if there was a need for me to be in New York, it only takes a few hours to get there."

"It's not something we have to decide today," he said. The dark room with the concentration of light from the fireplace continued to add an intimate glow to our conversation. I sat up and put my arms around my knees. Always thoughtful, Miles put his shirt around my shoulders, keeping his arm around me, leaning his head against mine.

"What other things?" I asked softly.

"Too much for a discussion tonight," he said, standing and offering his hand for me to follow. I looked at it for a minute, trying to decide if I was ready to let this conversation be over. Would we be able to revisit it again soon?

Taking his hand, he helped me up, then held me. "Everyone I hold dear in my life lives here," I said. "No matter the time frame, Nana doesn't have that long. I would never forgive myself if I got the call that she'd passed and I hadn't been here for the last portion of her life. She's the only real family I have."

"Death has a strange way of redefining life, doesn't it?" he said quietly as he picked up our discarded clothes and turned off the fireplace. "Mind if I spend what's left of the night?"

"Yeah, twist my arm," I said, following him to The Library.

It seemed perfectly natural when Jordan and Brandan came into the kitchen the following morning to find Miles and I had breakfast almost ready. "Look at you guys," Jordan said, kissing my cheek. "What a nice surprise!"

"She told me she could cook," Miles said, "but she didn't properly explain that she was a gourmet chef who can start with nothing except an open refrigerator door, study the contents, then two minutes later start whipping up mouth-watering dishes. This morning we're having Crème Brule French Toast with Drunken Strawberries, broiled, brown sugar grapefruit – and wait 'til you taste it! You guys may want to keep her around."

"Hopefully *someone* wants to," I said under my breath.

Miles and Brandan exchanged a look that I couldn't read, but it didn't matter. I was happy and had no intention of looking for trouble. I'd made it this far. The highly polished granite countertop in the kitchen now held a feast, and we enjoyed companionable banter as we sat on the surrounding stools sharing stories.

"So, Brandan, doesn't your hair get in the way of your work?" I asked, more in the way of teasing him for his long locks that curled from an obvious morning shower.

"No more so than yours." We all laughed. "I've actually often envied the way you hold yours up with a pencil. Mine's not long enough," he said, trying to imitate the knot I so often found mine wound in. While we laughed about different ways he could hold up his curls, Miles got a phone call. I could hear a woman's voice speaking, but I couldn't make out her words.

CHAPTER FIFTEEN

For the first time since we'd met, I saw him truly angry. A storm cloud of irritation washed over his face. "When?" he barked.

We all sat silently as he started pacing, listening to whatever distasteful words were being spoken. "Where is he now?"

"On my way," he said. His chest rose with an effort to draw in a deep breath.

"What is it?" I wanted to know, but I didn't want to take his focus off whatever was causing such concern. As though reorienting to his surroundings, he looked around the table and apologized. "I've gotta go." He leaned over to kiss my cheek. "Thank you for a delicious breakfast." It was done absently, and I don't think he was aware he had shown that display of affection, but I hated that he was this agitated over something that was none of my business, and there was nothing I could do to ease his distress.

"Anything I can do?" Brandan asked, an inaudible communication passing between them.

"Thanks, I got this one."

He was gone. We were each lost in our own thoughts at the sudden turn of events. Bless her heart, Jordan must've known I was anxious to know what was going on. "Any idea what that was about?" she asked Brandan.

"Nope," he said, clearing the half-empty plates from the counter and loading the dishwasher. He put his hand on my shoulder. "If I had any words that would help you understand, I'd share them," he said to me. "Unfortunately, I know about as much as you do."

"Thank you, that means a lot."

Jordan looked at me sympathetically and squeezed my hand. "Men," she said with a wink. "What are we gonna do with them?"

"I don't know, but you're doing a pretty good job finding out," he said to her.

"Hmmm," she said seductively. "I'll keep trying."

"I'm sorry about what happened, Jeni," he said. "Not necessarily the way you want to start your day."

His sympathetic kindness brought tears to my eyes. *Good grief, get yourself together, girl. You'll understand in due time.*

"If you guys have it covered here, I'm gonna straighten up and go see Nana."

"Sure, and thanks again for that incredible breakfast. I'm excited to have you here to teach me some of your secrets."

"Thank you both for letting me stay. I couldn't have planned this better. The setting, the place for Nana, the people you found to take care of her, it's all perfect."

I spent a good part of the afternoon with Nana until she fell asleep. Miriam assured me this was her routine, so I slipped out and tried to concentrate on a small ad campaign I'd taken on. When I hadn't heard from Miles by the end of the day, I finally broke down and texted.

Everything okay?

Lame, but I didn't know what else to say. It was the first time he hadn't stopped by to see Nana that I knew of. I wanted contact, wanted him to tell me what was going on. Was this part of the *"other things involved that we've never talked about"*? My curiosity was running rampant, and I wanted to know something, anything.

It didn't take him long to respond. *Sorry I ran out like that. Some personal stuff I had to take care of. I'll try to explain it soon. In the meantime, thanks for last night, thanks for breakfast. I enjoyed them both immensely (or was that intensely?) ;)*

There was a certain satisfaction from his response. I wasn't going to fall apart and take any of this personally. He obviously has a life outside of us, but my nature hated to be left in the dark. I was good about not borrowing trouble that didn't belong to me, but for those people I loved, I was a fighter and a protector. I loved Miles. He could take care of himself, but I wanted to stand by his side when he did it. According to Brandan, he'd been through a lot, and I'd never be able to thank him enough for his care and genuine concern for Nana, especially those months when I hadn't been here.

The leather-topped desk in my room was a perfect place to concentrate on my projects, although I was finding there weren't many places in the area that didn't inspire me. I'd become adept at working in twenty-five minute spurts, taking a five-minute break to get up and move, and then get back to the task at hand. It kept my thought processes fresh, and I wasn't fatigued at the end of a busy workday. Everything that needed to be done was completed online, and at times when human contact was necessary or it was easier to have it described in a live setting, we just set up a FaceTime chat or a Skype call, and work continued smoothly.

The next day after a productive morning, I called back to the cottage to let Miriam know I would give her a break at lunchtime and take Nana for an hour. Jordan and Brandan had ten acres, and I hadn't done a lot of exploring. I knew there was an old cemetery that adjoined the upper boundary of the property, and Jordan had told me about an area they'd cleared behind the cottage to the west for picnics. I packed a light lunch and went in search of it so I knew where it was before I got Nana.

A canopy of trees enshrined a space about twenty feet by thirty feet. The gentle breeze rustled the leaves at the top to provide a natural symphony, and toward the upper left section of this mountain oasis was a unique table with attached benches on each of its sides. The air was calm at ground level, and I felt confident the classic red-and-white checkered cloth would stay under the picnic basket until I retrieved my lunchtime guest.

The sizeable, rounded wicker basket was the color of softened suede and had two large wooden roses the color of currants attached on one side. The food I'd prepared was from recipes I'd learned at my grandmother's knee. I'd decided to bring small china plates, silverware, linen napkins, candles with holders, and crystal glasses. This would be a once-in-a-lifetime moment, and paper or plastic would not have sufficed.

Nana was in a chattering mood when I got to her enchanted home in the scenic setting that overlooked the water. Miriam had prepared her for my arrival, and she was like a kid promised a trip to an amusement part. She still liked to go places, and my chest clutched to see her child-like excitement over a temporary escape. I understood that her desire to be out would fade in time, so I wanted to provide opportunities while her mind was still able to appreciate small excursions.

We held hands the last part of the hike. Burrowing animals had taken their toll on the terrain, and I didn't want her to fall. I paused for effect as we entered the enclosure with air that smelled like paradise to see if she had any appreciation for where we were. Its splendor took my breath in this place where sunshine lingered and bees hummed, and I hoped she would be equally impressed.

She looked at the towering trees enclosing our eating area, and I wasn't disappointed when she said, almost with awe, "How did you ever find this place again? I figured you'd forgotten."

"Have we been here before?" I asked, trying to enter her world of memories.

"Of course we have. Your father and I used to bring you here when you were very young. There was a man who lived on the other side of the rise that built tiny houses everywhere. You brought your dolls and would play for hours."

Whether her memories were actual recollections or places her mind was now imagining, it was entertaining to spend time with her and hear the stories. Many of them were family stories I'd heard before, but some were not. Her tales were often intricate, and periodically sparked my imagination when I was working. I came by my creative abilities honestly. Nana had a fascinating ingenuity, and even as a child I was aware my friends envied me because I was blessed with a grandmother who could tell enthralling stories, and because of the treats she always had on hand.

If only for this moment in time, I'd be forever grateful I'd made the decision to be here. Quality time with loved ones happens when there is quantity time available, and these past few days wouldn't have been possible were I living on the other side of the country. We shared stories as we nibbled on chicken and rice salad with pine nuts, watermelon, and fresh apple pie. On some level her anecdotes were intimate, even though she believed she was sharing with my mother. I didn't mind substituting for that position and hearing what I believed to be honest details that her long-term memory was able to recall.

Pine needles crunched under our feet as we headed back to her cottage, and pungent smells that reminded me of our home at Christmastime rose faintly to tease my senses. In one hand I carried the picnic basket Brandan had given Jordan for one of their dates, and Nana held on tightly to the crook of my other arm. My heart hurt with love for this woman, and the other woman whom we had both loved whose presence now walked between us. I knew to my core she would've been proud of my decision to be here.

Jordan talked to me while I put everything away, hand washing and drying the sterling and crystal, and putting the food containers in the dishwasher. Everything was there except the spoons. Could I possibly have dropped them? Left them? Just as I was about to mention it, Jordan asked in a low voice, "Have you heard from Miles since he left so abruptly?"

"I feel like we're sharing secrets," I teased, "but nothing of any substance. He told me he was sorry, told me he'd tell me about it sometime, but, no, not really anything else."

"How can you stand it?" she asked, starting to pace. "I'd be going nuts. I hate being left in the dark. I'm not even involved with him and it's driving me crazy. I'd track Brandan down and hold him around the neck 'til I had answers." Our eyes met as the wheels started turning in both our brains.

"Come on, Jeni, we're plotters, it's what we do best. Don't you want to find out?"

"Of course I do, but how do you propose I do that?"

"You gave up your world and moved out here. You'll never convince me he wasn't a huge part of your decision. So you go have a face-to-face with him, what else?"

"Seriously? Would *you* do that?"

"Darned tootin' I would. I've known, probably longer that either of you, that there was something out of the ordinary between you. Sometimes we just have to figure out what it is we want, then decide what we're going to do to get it."

"Can we find out where he's working today?" I asked, seriously considering her idea.

"I probably wouldn't go where there are a lot of guys around. I'd go to his house."

"Ugh. That thought kinda makes me sick to my stomach."

"Why? He comes here all the time."

"There's something a little scary about just showing up at his house."

"You? Where's my fearless friend? Nothing scares you. You want him, go find out how he feels. I imagine the best place to do that would be his house. Have you ever been there before?"

"No, I don't even know where he lives except that he's got a house in Sugarloaf."

"Getting an address is no problem. Come on, don't you wanna know?"

"I'm the one who usually talks *you* into hair-brained schemes. What would I possibly say to him?"

We spent the next half hour coming up with different scenarios, each one making my heart beat a little faster at the possible outcomes. But I kept wondering what I had to lose. Jordan was right, I'd never been the shy, retiring type. There was no question I thought we had a good chance for a future, but something had to change. I was ready to take it to the next level and find out what those *"other things involved that we've never talked about because you being here was never a possibility"* could conceivably be.

"Okay, I'll swallow my pride and do it. If I haven't heard from him by dinnertime, I'll head up there. Hopefully he'll stop by to see Nana and this will all be moot."

"You go find your tightest jeans, I'll go find an address. Damn, I wish I could be a fly on the wall," she laughed, heading up the stairs.

When the afternoon came and went with no sign of Miles, I started drawing up my courage to pay him a visit. I knew what we had was real on a lot of levels, but I also knew there were large chunks of missing information. Brandan and Jack had worked with him for years and knew him to be the best of the best, and I had seen his care and concern for Nana and for me, so I wasn't deluding myself about what a nice guy he was. But after the night we'd had, it caused some sad places in my heart that needed healing after he'd walked out so abruptly the next morning. I was ready to find out if he was willing to shine some light into the darkness his absence had created.

CHAPTER SIXTEEN

Blood surging through my veins was the only sound I heard as I pulled in front of the address Jordan had given me. Sugarloaf was a sparsely populated mountain town, but the modest homes were well kept, and I could see why anyone would be enamored with it. More of a residential area than Nederland, it was located close enough to Boulder that it would be an easy drive to find anything you might need. There was something appealing to find this was where he'd not only grown up, but where he chose to stay.

I parked across the street, taking deep breaths to settle the shaking that seemed to have taken hold of me. Opening the car door, I was surprised how difficult it was to maneuver my hands to accomplish even so simple a task. What was the matter with me? What's the worst that could happen here? If it upset him because I showed up, then we didn't have the connection I thought we did. It was such a sleepy community, there'd probably not been a crime committed here in years, so I thought nothing of leaving my purse on the floor of the front seat and not locking the car doors. I didn't want anything in my hands to distract me.

There was a newer model, deep blue SUV parked in the driveway as I crossed the street. *Crap, what if he had company?* I hesitated slightly as the front door opened and an attractive woman with a young child on her hip started to step out. Miles was in the doorway looking inside when she leaned in to kiss him on the cheek, closed the door behind her, and started toward the parked car.

What if that was his wife and child? Was that possible? Had I really been incredibly blind? What a stupid thought, of course he wasn't married. He'd told me several times he wasn't. Yeah, right, like that mattered. Stop it right now. Brandan or Callie or Jack would have said something. Why hadn't I listened to my gut and stayed away? Was I really standing here arguing with myself? I stood frozen in place, wondering what to do now, trying to come up with some other reasonable explanation.

As she headed down the stairs to the driveway, she noticed me standing there. When our eyes met, what appeared to be a genuine smile crossed her face. Not having the least ability to explain what I was doing there, I turned and hurried to my car, clumsily trying to get the door opened. What a fool I was, and what a fool she must think me to turn tail and run like that. I'm sure they'd laugh about it, whoever she was.

I got my purse to the seat and bumbled to get the keys out. When I finally straightened to put them in the ignition, the welcoming smile was still plastered to the face that was right by my window. I had no option but to roll down the window to acknowledge her. "You looking for Miles?" she asked in a melodious voice.

Having no idea how to answer her question, I looked down at the smiling little girl who was fidgeting in her arms, and who happened to be the spitting image of Miles. My eyes narrowed as bile rose in my throat. I wondered if this paragon of a mother would look as pretty and sweet if I threw up on her.

Looking at me, then looking at the angelic child, a larger smile crossed her face. "Forgive my manners," she said, extending her free hand in greeting. "I'm Maggie, Miles' sister." Was it possible she had understood my thoughts? "This is my daughter, Harper."

"She's beautiful," I said as cherubic hands reached for me.

"She doesn't usually take to strangers. That's interesting. She looks just like Miles, doesn't she?" she continued, confirming my suspicions. "And you are...?"

Realizing she had spoken to me, I found an honest smile and said, "I'm Jeni. I'm a friend of Miles'."

"I wondered if you were," she said. "Miles has told me quite a bit about you." *Really?* I wanted to ask. He hadn't told me anything about her except she was bedridden during her pregnancy when their mom was dying. But why did I get the feeling she was up to mischief?

She opened my car door and said, "Please, don't leave. Miles would be so disappointed if you came all this way and then left before you got a chance to see him. Come on, he'll be delighted." She took my hand, and I followed reluctantly up flower-trimmed stairs toward the immaculately kept, ranch-style home. He must've seen us, because he was standing in the open doorway, arms crossed, and I couldn't read his absent expression.

"Look who I found," Maggie said, an impish grin playing across her face.

Miles looked at our entwined hands as I tried to politely disentangle them. "I was in the neighborhood?" I said, trying to inject some humor into the situation.

"She thought I was your wife," she said.

I gasped. "No, I didn't!" My mouth was agape. "I never said that!" I said, looking between them.

"No, she didn't say that, but you should've seen the look on her face when she saw Harper. She didn't know what to think about the resemblance."

"I thought you liked me?" I whispered to her, choking back a laugh as she tried to drag me further.

"Oh, honey, I do. Miles has a heap of explaining to do, and he doesn't have very long to do it because Runner will be home any minute," she said, very pointedly at her brother.

"Runner?" I asked. In all of my imaginings, this scenario hadn't been one that presented itself.

"Sure didn't mean to put you on the spot," she said, kissing my cheek and waving as she headed for her car. "Sometimes he can be so butt-headed and needs a little push. I just shoved him."

Looking away from the attractive, delightful woman who was his sister, my eyes met his as the fading sunlight gave everything an etherial glow, casting us in a cocoon of fantasy. A stunning smile spread across his face as he held out his hand for me to take. "Welcome to my home, Jeni. I'm glad you're here."

Feeling the sincerity in his words, I stepped into the living room. It was spectacular. Masculine, immaculate, nothing out of place, blacks and browns with accents here and there of navy with a splash of blood red, I looked around with admiration at what a welcoming atmosphere this was, and how homey it felt. The vaulted ceilings followed the roofline with exposed beams crossing the length of the main floor. Windows in all the peaks and on most of the walls let the fading sun in to reflect off most of the surfaces. "Well, blow me over with a feather," I breathed in awe, stepping in further so he could close the door. "I'm so impressed."

"Callie helped me after mom died. I wanted to stay here, but every room, every corner, every piece of furniture reminded me of her. It was pretty painful, so I enlisted Callie's aid and we made it *my* home, changed it up completely. Jack and Brandan helped me redo the kitchen and bathrooms, opened the ceilings to the rafters. I bought all new furniture. So you like it?" he asked as though looking for my approval.

"I love it, Miles. It's so you, so inviting, so I'd-never-want-to-leave-here gorgeous."

"I'm glad," he said, opening his arms. I stepped into them, feeling like I was where I belonged, now glad beyond measure I'd let Jordan talk me into this hair-brained scheme.

"We need to talk, Jeni," he said, leading me into the magnificent kitchen. It was a shock to see this kind of detail in this little village on the side of a mountain.

"I'm all ears." I took a seat at the kitchen counter, trying to soak it all in. "Talk away."

The front door slammed open hard enough to make me jump. "Hey, Dad, is it okay with you if Rusty spends the night? His mom said it was okay."

A hundred things went through my mind as a young boy with wavy brown hair and piercing blue eyes came into the kitchen, setting a baseball and glove on the midnight blue granite. His face radiated intelligence, and I estimated him to be about ten. When he saw me, he smiled and extended his hand. "Hi, I'm Runner. This is my friend Rusty," he said, pointing behind him to a young man with streaks of cinnamon coloring in his hair, and a profusion of freckles painted across his nose and cheeks. They appeared to be the same age, but he was obviously much shyer than the outgoing Runner, and Rusty merely nodded in my direction.

"I'm Jeni," I said with a genuine smile, shaking his hand. "I'm a friend of your dad's." His dad – minor little thing we had yet to talk about. I'd save the shock for later.

"You *are*?" He asked. "You're the first *'friend'* my dad's ever brought to the house. Nice to meet you." I'm not sure I'd ever met a more polite young man, and I would swear Miles actually blushed.

"You know those don't go there," he said, nodding to the mitt and ball. "Take them to your room and wash up for dinner. Aunt Maggie made you some Carbonara. And it's all right with me if Rusty stays, as long as it's okay with his mom."

"Thanks, Dad! Nice to meet you, Jeni!" he called as he opened a door and ran down a flight of stairs. "Oh, and Dad?" he said, coming halfway up. "If Jeni wants to see what you did in my room, I wouldn't mind at all if you showed her." He was off again, Rusty trailing more sedately behind.

I looked at Miles, then ran my hand over the smooth, cool countertop, noticing the flecks of mica that were now shining golden in the last rays of the day. I slid my hands across its surface until my face rested on my arm, then I burst into laughter. I'm not sure what he was thinking my reaction would be, but I was certain from the look on his face this was not it.

"What's so funny?" He stepped up behind me and put a hand on my back. "Why are you laughing?"

"When I came up here tonight, I was terrified of what might happen. I didn't have a clue. I hadn't heard from you, and Jordan made me swallow my pride and come face reality. In my wildest dreams, in all of the circumstances she and I conjured up, you having a captivatingly polite young man for a son never entered the picture, wasn't even in the realm of possibility."

I sat up abruptly and turned to him. "Listen to me, Miles. I've asked you several times before and I believed you. I'm not sure how I can handle it if you're married. Do you have any other surprises for me?" I asked almost desperately.

"Jeni, Jeni, Jeni," he said, standing between my legs and wrapping me in his arms as I continued to sit on the stool. He pulled me close and rested his head against my hair. "His mother and I see each other every few years whether we have to or not," he said in a faraway voice. "I have sole custody of Runner, she saw him last Christmas for an hour. There's no one else."

"That's tragic! That brings up so many *other* questions. But I have to ask first, why didn't you ever tell me? That actually really hurts."

"It didn't have anything to do with you and me. The day I met you in Jordan's kitchen, I felt like I'd been sucker punched. In my entire life, I'd never reacted that way to another human being. I didn't believe in love at first sight, but I sure as hell didn't know what else to call it. Then you taunted me, almost like a dare, to tell me not to fall in love with you because you were going to be gone soon."

"Oh, my God," I said into his chest. "Miles, I was so in love with you I couldn't breathe. I was protecting myself, thinking you were too good to be true."

"Whatever was going on, I couldn't do that to Runner. I could never expose him to another woman who would never be around, who would only be a temporary fixture in his life. My mom took care of him until she got sick, and he lost her, too. It wasn't fair to him to meet you, it wasn't fair to me, so I shut myself off from you. We both saw how well that worked," he laughed, hugging me even tighter.

"Miles . . ."

"Listen, the boys will be up soon. We have so many things to talk about, but they can all wait. Now that you know, it will make things so much easier, and I won't feel like I'm lying to you."

"Wait, does Jordan know?"

"I don't think so. Brandan and Jack know, of course, but everyone's been so protective of him, not many people except those we've been close to for years have any idea. And Callie knows since she spent so much time up here helping me change things up."

"How old is he?"

"Almost eleven."

"Really, were you a teenager?"

"No, his mom and I were friends in college, I was twenty-two when he was born. Listen, that's a long, involved story. I'll have to have a few shots under my belt to tell you that one," he said as tromping footsteps could be heard coming up the stairs.

"All washed up. You staying for dinner, Jeni?" Runner asked invitingly.

Miles nodded, indicating it was my choice. "I'd love to! Mind if I wash my hands in the kitchen sink?"

"Go right ahead. I'll get the plates and we can sit on the deck and turn on the fire pit."

Without being asked, Runner got down four glasses and went to the stainless steel refrigerator. "You want lemonade or iced tea?"

"Lemonade, thanks."

After pouring four glasses, he and Rusty each took two and headed to the back porch. "Need my help for anything, Dad?"

"No, I got it. Jeni can bring the napkins and silverware and I'll bring the plates."

"I don't know about you," I said, rolling forks and spoons in paper napkins, "but I feel like I just fell into the Twilight Zone. I know we won't be able to talk, but I want you to know I think he's an amazing kid, and, if possible, I love you more than I did when I was dragged to the door by your outlandish sister."

His laughter echoed. "You think *you're* a character? I'm not sure anyone can hold a candle to Maggie in the tell-it-like-it-is department."

He stopped in front of me, loving me with his eyes. "I'm sorry you found out this way. I'm sorry things snowballed like this. After you told me you weren't leaving, I would've told you yesterday, but then something happened at school that blew so many things apart. Give me a little time, I'll do what I can to help you understand. There's still a lot to tell you."

"More kids?" I asked.

"Heavens no!" he said.

"Miles?"

"Yes, Jeni?" he said, standing close to me without touching. "They can see us, you know, so I'm not going to kiss you like I want."

"Miles?"

His indulgent smile crossed his face.

"This has obviously been a complete shock to my system. I'm standing strong for the next punch, but I have to ask. Do you love me?"

CHAPTER SEVENTEEN

He didn't answer at first. His breath was close enough to brush my cheek, but still he didn't touch me, only with his eyes. "I'm sorry I haven't let you know without you having to ask. I've obviously been conflicted. I didn't want to promise you any part of me if you were going to be nothing but a wishful fantasy the next morning. But, yes, Jeni, I do. I knew beyond a doubt when I saw you with Charlotte Rose, but truth be told, I probably have since the day we met. Will that hold you over until we can talk?"

My eyes fixed on him in watering adoration. "As long as that's truth, I can deal with anything."

He headed toward the sliding doors leading to the back, and Runner immediately opened it. Little rascals, they *had* been watching. It felt similar to the times we'd look up and find Nana standing there. I'd have fun figuring out creative ways for us to be alone.

The flames from the torches and the fire pit illuminated the luscious lawn enough for the boys to toss and chase a football. Maggie's dinner had been simple but delicious, but the joy of the evening came in listening to the interaction between Miles and Runner. There was tangible respect for each other, and Runner's sense of humor was ignited with his continued banter with his father.

We laughed until our sides hurt. Strong barbs of affection for this child pierced my heart, tugging painfully. How could a mother not want to share in this incredible life she had helped create? In just a few hours, he had so impressed me it would be impossible to forget him. Knowing Miles had been the major influence in his young life caused a rush of emotion, somehow fueling my deepest, most desperate desires, and a moment of pure envy swept over me.

He pulled his phone from his pocket and started texting. "I know how close you and Jordan are. I'm going to tell Brandan he might want to tell her about Runner before you get home."

"Tell me what's going on in your head that you'd think of that," I asked.

"When you get home, you're gonna want to talk to her about what happened tonight. I know how girls plot," he laughed. "I don't care if she knows, but it may be best if it comes from Brandan. Otherwise, she'll think he was keeping secrets from her."

"That's pretty perceptive of you. And you're absolutely right. It will be much better for them if he tells her himself." Leaning and squeezing his hand, I said sincerely, "Thank you."

Was his heart constricting like mine as we stared at each other? "There's so much I want to tell you. This makes things so much easier."

"Where does he stay when you're with me?"

"Maggie has an eight-year-old son named Caleb. He and Runner are close, close enough they don't realize they have separate houses. I made them a bed that looks like a pirate ship, and Runner enjoys being there so it's no hardship when he has to stay. Maggie's been an involved part of his life since he was born."

"How did he get the name Runner?"

Miles closed his eyes and leaned his head back slightly. "Long story, I'll give you the condensed version." His eyes now followed the football back and forth across the yard, finally settling on his son. "His mom was a runner in college, hours a day. When she got pregnant, she was furious it was going to inhibit her lifestyle. I spent weeks talking her out of having an abortion, but she really didn't want anything to do with having a baby."

"Were you married?"

"No, we were good friends, but we weren't in love with each other. She agreed we could live together, and if I really wanted to have a baby, she'd try hard to be a mom." His voice was low enough that the boys couldn't hear what he was telling me. "I was thrilled. Even though I was young, I was idealistic enough to believe we could make it work. We'd been close since we met a few years earlier.

"As he grew inside her, we could see his feet moving, and I'd tease her, trying to give her a bond to him, and tell her he was going to be a runner just like his mom. The more races she had to miss, the more she resented him. Even as a baby when he was asleep, his feet were constantly moving. From the day he was born, I always thought of him as Runner. Maggie, of course, loved the name, and he's been called that from the beginning."

"Is that his given name?"

Miles laughed. "No, Coulson Lucas Jeffries. Maggie had just gotten married, and her husband Luke and I were, still are, good friends. Coulson was my best friend in college, and he went on to play professional football. We see him every now and then, and he takes Runner under his wing and gives him pointers. Has a real affinity for him."

"God, Miles, it would be hard not to. He's one of the neatest kids I've met."

"I'm glad you think so." Looking at Runner he said, "I'm amazed every day that he's mine. He has the most compassionate heart. I'm so proud of him."

"It's a testament to you."

"I had a lot of help from my mom and Maggie."

"Where's Runner's mom now?"

"Denver."

"Hey, Dad, catch!" Runner ran way back as Miles stood with a smile on his face. A torpedo shot through the air and was placed perfectly between Miles' waiting hands.

"Good grief," I teased, "have the scouts found him yet?"

"Actually, he likes baseball more than football at this point, but he's got lots of time. I figure it helps him wear off some of that energy he has such an abundance of."

The blazing red sky had given way to nighttime. Without city lights, thousands of stars blossomed in the darkness. "Time to call it a night, guys," Miles said to the boys.

"I'm gonna go, too." I gathered plates and cups. "Thank you for letting me share your dinner," I said to no one in particular, opening the dishwasher and putting the dishes inside.

"You don't need to do that," Miles said.

"No big deal. It's the least I can do."

"Will we see you again?" Runner asked. He and Rusty grabbed a chocolate chip cookie from a plate on the counter, and I wondered if Maggie had made those as well.

"I'd love that," I said, looking at Miles.

"Good cookie, Dad. Much better than the last batch," he said as they headed down the stairs.

"I'm gonna walk Jeni to her car. I'll be right back. Get in your pajamas and brush your teeth, I'll be down in a few."

He opened my car door. "I know it's been a roller coaster tonight, but you handled it beautifully."

"Hard not to be impressed, you should be proud."

"He's always friendly, but he doesn't usually take to strangers that way. I'm glad you stopped by."

"I didn't have much choice." I caught his eye and smirked. "Jordan was insistent."

We were both smiling when he bent and covered my mouth with his. He pulled me close and, for just a moment, transported us to our own erotic world of which only he and I were aware. "I promise I'll stop by tomorrow. Right now, I have a feeling that someone's straining his neck to see what's going on out here." Tucking my hair behind my ear, he placed a chaste kiss on my lips, then took the stairs two at a time. I chuckled to think about their adrenalin rush as two young boys were scrambling right now to make it back downstairs before they got caught.

"Do Runner and James Gabriel know each other?" I asked the next afternoon when Miles joined us in the Manor kitchen.

"Yeah, I brought him a couple of times when we were working on the cottage before Nana got here." He and Brandan exchanged a smile.

"Where was I?" Jordan asked, somewhat incredulous. "How could I not have known any of this?"

"You weren't looking, you didn't ask," Brandan said.

"I'm a lawyer. I pride myself on being observant."

"If you'll recall," he said to her kindly, "you were involved in your own discoveries while we worked on the cottage, and it wasn't my story to tell."

"And it's not like I was hiding him," Miles said. "Because he's had some rough life circumstances, including my mother's recent death, I'm pretty protective of not getting him too emotionally involved with people who are going to be out of his life in a hurry. She was his caregiver until she got sick. And might I remind you, counselor, you were in a big hurry to hightail it back to New York yourself."

"That's true, but my powers of observation are keen, and to coin Jeni's phrase, you could've blown me over with a feather when Brandan told me. I couldn't imagine how Jeni must've been handling it."

"Like a champ," he said.

Jordan and I cracked up. "Yeah, yesterday afternoon as we debated the pros and cons of going up there, this didn't enter either of our minds. But I'll never be sorry for how it turned out," I said quietly.

"Thank you," he whispered.

"Is Runner too old for the Carousel of Happiness?" I asked.

Everyone chimed in that no one is too old for the Carousel. "I've told James Gabriel several times that

I'd take him," I said. "Would it be terribly presumptuous of me to invite Runner to go with us? Maybe take Nana? I think she might enjoy it."

"If you don't mind if I tag along, I think he'd really like that. I haven't taken him since it opened when he was six, *and* he couldn't stop talking about *you* this morning," Miles said, looking at me. "It will cover all kinds of bases."

I blushed. "I thought he was pretty neat. I'd like to spend more time with him."

As though we were the only two in the room, we stared at each other. "They're at it again," Brandan laughed.

We were all interrupted when the basement door closed and we turned to see Nana standing there. "Where did you come from?" I asked, looking at the others, then taking her by the hand and leading her to the counter. "Want something to drink? Tell me how you got here."

"I walked, how else would I have gotten here? What a silly question, Jeni."

It always made my heart rush when she seemed to know who I was. While Jordan and I talked to her about what she'd been doing, Miles and Brandan quietly went to the basement. It puzzled us all how she mysteriously appeared, and this was the first time to my knowledge anyone had actually seen where she'd come from. We called back to the cottage to let Miriam know Nana was here. She was shocked because she'd seen Nana asleep in her chair just ten minutes earlier. The guys came back, shaking their heads, apparently none the wiser.

Miles and I walked her back to the cottage, letting her know we would take her on an excursion the next day. The look of sheer joy on her face warmed my heart, and it didn't matter how long she would remember the conversation, her anticipation was priceless. Miles and I snooped around the cottage to see if there was anywhere obvious she could be escaping from. The alarms on the doors and windows were functional, and it was still a mystery.

"Nana," I asked quietly, "can you show me where you go when you leave here?"

"I go to see you at the big house," she said, matter of factly.

"But how do you get there?" I didn't want to get frustrated with her, but it might become an issue in the future.

"I can't figure out why you keep asking me that. I walk. That's it, I just walk, usually with Henry." She was getting anxious, and the conversation was over for now.

Miles touched my arm, indicating for me not to press it any further. "Okay, Nana, we'll see you tomorrow. Miles and I will come pick you up."

Helpless wisps of hair blew this way and that on some mysterious wind as we walked back to the Manor. "It's usually the wind that keeps people away," Miles said loud enough for me to hear. "Not the snow, but the bone-chilling wind that howls through any available opening, regardless of what you do to keep it at bay. It'll get to you a lot quicker than the cold."

"Think about what it was like for the people who settled this town. It must've driven some of them mad."

"Probably," he said reflectively. "Although I think you had to be a little mad to come up here in the first place to settle such a wilderness. All this time later, there's still a remoteness to it."

The sage green SUV delivered itself with timely precision in front of the cottage. We were waiting with childlike anticipation for the coming adventure, each for our own reason. They were excited because we were going to the Carousel of Happiness, I was excited not only to have an outing with Miles, but to be spending more time with Runner, an integral part of Miles' life and a fascinating young person.

Nana rode the short trip in the front, with me in the back between the boys. They got along well, and we were in high spirits when we arrived. Something in the Carousel triggered her memory, because Nana told us her father let her ride over and over until she'd ridden each horse. There was only one horse here, an Indian pony, but there were thirty-four other hand-carved animals. Some she rode for the entire rotation, some she had fun moving from one to another while the music played. Miles, of course, helped her mount and dismount each one, and by the time we were done, I was exhausted. I couldn't imagine how she was still going.

It wasn't more than a few steps from the Carousel of Happiness to Buffalo Bill's Coffee and Confections next door. Three original train cars from the Buffalo Bill Wild West Show had been painted red and put together to make this unique restaurant, and the boys were anxious for ice cream to end our play date.

Running with childish exuberance, they raced ahead as I followed to purchase whatever refreshment might please their fancy.

Through the window I could see Miles walking up the ramp at a sedate pace, my grandmother holding his arm as though on a lighthearted outing. He laughed at the things she said, and the joyous look on her face would stay with me for a long time. We were creating special memories, and there wasn't a day I hadn't been thankful to be here. We sat on couches in the caboose and ate our ice cream, the boys being polite, listening respectfully as Nana reminisced.

"Are you familiar with the Caribou Ranch recording studio outside of town?" Miles asked.

"Wasn't that where anybody who was anybody in the early '70s used to record?" I asked. "Billy Joel, John Denver, Jerry Garcia, Grace Slick, Chicago? Yeah, I've heard of it," I said teasingly.

We shared a smile. "Did you know that the couches we're sitting on came from there?"

"Really?" I said, irresistibly interested. "Good Lord, Miles, can you imagine the stories they could tell?"

That ended any one-on-one interaction we had until we dropped Nana back at the cottage. As he got out to help her into the house, he turned to us in the back.

"Don't anyone move, I'll be right back." She patted his face as he left her at the door, Miriam waving to us as she took over from Miles.

CHAPTER EIGHTEEN

Backing out, he pulled in front of Madeline Manor. "Do you have any plans for the evening, ma'am?" he asked me formally.

"Not that I'm aware of, sir."

"I've checked with April, and she says James Gabriel is welcome to come with us. Runner and I would like to know if you need to check with anyone, and would you join us for dinner at Casa Bonita in Denver?"

"I'd love to! What is it?"

"Their food wouldn't make them famous, well, unless it's to talk about how tasteless it is, but it's an experience everyone should try at least once. Runner and I haven't been in years, and April says James Gabriel's never been."

"I'm totally game, thank you! Do I need to change clothes?"

"Nope, you're over-dressed, if anything. But you do need to sit up front now. I didn't want Nana to think we were going somewhere without her. You never know what she's aware of and what she's not."

"I love your heart," I said quietly as I buckled in the front as we headed out. "Thank you for your beautiful care of her. Today was extraordinary, and whether she remembers it tomorrow or not, the joy of it will last with me for a long time."

He squeezed my hand. "You know it's my pleasure."

The trip was non-stop cheerful chatter. "Hey, Jeni, do you know what those things are along the side of the road?"

Runner was pointing to pipes that stood out of the ground every quarter mile or so. They had cone-shaped caps that looked like pointed mushrooms, and were painted in bright colors, all of them different.

When we passed the third one, I didn't have a clue. Looking at Miles, I grinned and said, "Those are gnome homes."

Miles let out a bark of laughter, and the boys weren't sure whether to take me seriously or not. "Really?" James Gabriel asked. "What's a gnome?"

"They're tiny people about four inches tall who have magical powers."

"Really?" he asked, somewhat incredulous.

"Really," Runner said, winking at me. "Thanks, Jeni, I've always wondered where they lived."

"Now you know."

Miles leaned over and squeezed my hand, and I was pleased when he didn't let go. As we pulled into what appeared to be an abandoned mall, my eyes rose to look at him.

"We drove an hour for this? It's a good thing I trust you," I said, looking at the empty stores that surrounded it. There was trash blowing throughout the parking lot that was mostly vacant except right in front of Casa Bonita, where it looked like a Wal-Mart on a Saturday afternoon.

"It doesn't look like much, but they've been in business for about forty years, and even though everything around them seems to be dying, they continue to thrive. The place is always packed, you'll see."

"You're gonna love it, Jeni," Runner said from the back seat. "Come on. It's really cool."

"Slow down, boys, wait for us."

"Yes, sir," they said in unison.

Miles took my hand as we walked across the parking lot, the boys bouncing up and down with anticipation. At the entry was a huge water feature where people were climbing and posing, and kids were trying to catch the overspray. The late afternoon sun was hidden behind a haze that made everything appear golden. "The fountain's interesting," I said, trying to find something encouraging to point out in this surreal setting.

"They shipped it in pieces from Mexico in the early 70s. Just think, right about the time they were jamming at Caribou Ranch, they were putting this fountain together."

The place was packed, and we were herded into lines to order buffet-style. The food came out to a counter with colorful blue, orange, and white mosaic tiles, reminding me of something you might see in Santa Fe. We each picked up our plates and stepped into the main part of the restaurant, and everything was transformed. Okay, now I saw its attraction. There was a feel of Mexico, and music and noise blared from every corner, with different rooms for young and old alike.

"Let's go up by the waterfall," Miles said over the din.

"*Yeah!*" the boys yelled and started running.

"Not necessarily someplace you'd want to come for a quiet, romantic date, but it's a lot of fun," Miles said close to my ear. "By the way, they're air vents for an underground water system, but – gnome homes · that was clever."

"Glad you enjoyed it," I said, giving him a quick kiss. "Good grief, this place is huge!"

"It's over fifty-thousand square feet. There are pirate caves and play rooms and game rooms and magic shows and shops, you name it. But my favorite part is the falls. Let's see if we can get a table near there."

Coming to the upper level, being pushed in a throng of bodies, it was evident we weren't the only ones who thought it was worth the trip. The boys were standing by a table, trays in hand, waiting for a couple who were leaving. "Look, Dad, we can watch them while we eat!" Runner called excitedly.

The waterfall appeared to be several stories high, and on one of the ledges were men twirling flaming batons. "It's over thirty feet to the water," Miles said. "They should be diving soon. It's impressive."

James Gabriel stood with his mouth agape. I set my plate down and went up behind him to look over the rail into the beautiful turquoise pool below that was churning as it came into contact with the water rushing from the falls. "Pretty neat, huh?" I asked, ruffling his hair.

"It's the coolest thing I've ever seen!" he said in awe.

Runner joined us, standing next to James Gabriel looking over the smooth wood fencing that prevents patrons from falling in. "My dad brought me here when I was a kid," he said, sounding so grown up. "I didn't think it would look as big, but it looks even bigger than I remember."

"Thanks for bringing me here," I said, putting my hand on his shoulder. He looked up at me and a broad smile split his face.

"Sure," he said, effervescently happy. "Let's eat!"

Between bites, we watched the performance of the divers, watched them fall from the cliffs, straight into the deep, swirling pool below.

"Is it the lighting, or are you feeling a little green?" Miles teased.

"I was just thinking that very thing. It's amazing to watch, but it would give me heart failure to fall into such a little bit of water."

"It's about fifteen feet deep, so there's plenty of room when they get there."

"Yeah, but it's the getting there that would do me in."

The roar of the water made it difficult to hear each other speak. A few minutes later a six-man mariachi band stopped by the table to serenade us. The boys were interested for a few minutes, then popped up to get closer to the rails again, caring only about the divers. Miles put an arm around me as we listened to the sweet love song they played, and there wasn't a part of this entire experience that wasn't being absorbed into some part of my being. As the band moved on to the next table, James Gabriel ran over to us, bouncing from one foot to the other.

"I gotta go to the bathroom," he said.

Smiling, Miles stood. "I'll take him. Will you keep an eye on Runner?"

"Of course. Won't let him out of my sight."

I stood with him at the railing, listening to the clapping as another diver hit the water. "You done with your dinner?" I asked as we turned back to the table.

"Yeah. Can we go to the pirate cave?"

"Sure, but let's wait 'til they get back. They'd never find us." Looking around, I leaned over so he could hear me, "Not sure they can find us in all of this confusion anyway."

Looking past me, the smile and color drained from his face. Turning to see what could possibly have caused his reaction, there was nothing but the crowding mass of people who wanted to be where we were, watching the divers. I was even more surprised as he took my hand and moved closer, and the vibrant young man became old beyond his years before my eyes. Putting his arm around my waist, he whispered, "Please?"

I had no idea what was going on, but he didn't have to ask me twice. I put my arm around him and pulled him close, trying to give him a smile of encouragement and strength. I'd find out soon enough.

"Hello, Runner," a delicate, stunning blonde said as she stopped in front of us.

"Ann," he said, nodding in her direction, his grasp around my waist growing imperceptibly tighter.

It immediately struck me how different his greeting of her was in comparison to the exuberant young man I had met at his home the other day. No warmth, no offer of a handshake, no light in his eyes, just a dull greeting of this exotic female.

She took her eyes from his face and turned toward me, extending her hand, "Hi, I'm Ann," the vision said in a voice matching her beauty. As our hands met in greeting she added, "I'm Runner's mother."

I'm not sure about my facial reaction, but I was quite certain she noticed as I jerked my hand from her grasp. Was Miles broken hearted when things didn't work out with her? She was breathtaking, and I hated her on sight, not because I was jealous, but anyone who could turn this boisterous young man who stood motionless in my embrace to such lifelessness could not be a good person. There was so much I suddenly wished Miles had told me.

"She's dad's fiancé," the small voice said next to me. *What did he just say?*

Disbelief crossed her face as she assessed me from my ponytail to my sneakers. When she looked at me like that, I felt inadequate, then remembered this was the woman who left her son because she didn't want to be a mother. I didn't give a rat's ass what she thought of me, every protective instinct in me came rushing to the fore as I pulled him closer.

"Good," she said. "I'm glad to see your dad's finally getting on with his life. It's been long enough." She didn't appear smug when she said it, but everything about her made my spirit hiss.

A young girl of about five ran up and threw her arms around Runner. "What are you doing here?" she asked in a singsong voice. "Did you see the divers? Aren't they cool?"

He hugged her with his free arm, his countenance softening slightly, and said, "My dad and I brought Jeni to dinner."

Ann took her by the hand, gently pulling her away.

"That's my half-sister, Rachel," Runner said.

Good God, were there more surprises? She hadn't wanted to be a mother to Runner, but she had a daughter who looked just like her who she was holding with affection? Anger rose to almost choke me. Never had I been happier to see someone as Miles and James Gabriel came up the ramp. Could he smell the anger that emanated from me? He had an immediate grasp of the situation as he stood on Runner's other side and put an arm around him, entwining it with mine. Having no clue of the thick tension around him, James Gabriel asked excitedly if they could go play video games. Miles understood the pleading look Runner gave him and gave them each money.

"Don't go anywhere but the arcade, understand?"

"Yes, sir," they called as they ran off. Runner stopped several feet away and turned. "Bye, Rachel," he said with a smile, then took off again.

If I hadn't loved him before, Runner solidified every kind thought I had about him in that simple, kind gesture. That he understood Rachel wasn't to blame for whatever ill will existed in this once-nuclear family was a testament to his father's heart and upbringing. I reached for Miles' hand, and was rewarded with him stepping closer to me, pulling me tight against him. I flushed with satisfaction.

"What brings you to such a public outing? I thought you hated crowds," he asked. Could she hear the contempt dripping in his voice?

"Alex's folks are in town. They've wanted to see this place for years. It just worked out we could all make it this trip." Rachel pulled free and went running off, and Ann turned to see where she was going. An older man scooped her up, and Ann smiled as she turned back to us.

"That's Alex's dad," she said to me.

"We're going to find the boys," Miles said, nodding, obviously not wanting to stay and socialize.

"Don't be rude, Miles, at least stay and say hello to Alex." Was she goading him?

Whatever I was expecting, I was glad Miles had his arm around me when the person who was obviously Alex planted a kiss firmly on Ann's lips. The woman was at least six inches taller than Ann with short dark hair and a muscular build, her subsequent smile seeming at once triumphant and taunting. There was a degree of claiming territory evident in the possessiveness of the action. Putting an arm around Ann, Alex nodded and said, "Hello, Miles."

"Alex," he nodded in recognition but without warmth. The older couple with Rachel walked up and, with sincere friendliness, said hello to Miles. Reeling with the surprise and implications of everything going on around me, I put on my fake smile and nodded to Alex and the older couple.

"Hi, I'm Jeni," I said. Having no idea why it was important to him but knowing Runner wanted them to believe it, I squeezed Miles a little tighter when I said, "I'm Miles' fiancé."

Alex's parents seemed honestly pleased with the news and offered their congratulations. Alex asked, "So when's the big day?"

Without missing a beat, Miles said, "Jeni moved here a few weeks ago from New York. I'm going to give her a month or so to acclimate, but we're hoping in about six weeks."

"You've just met then?" Ann asked.

"No, we've known each other a long time. Everything worked out recently for her to move here to be with Runner and me. He's very excited," he said pointedly.

"That's great," Alex's mom said, obviously welcoming the news. "It will be good for you both. Sorry to hear about your mother," she said to Miles. "I know how close you were."

"Thank you. It was a great loss." Looking at me to signal our time was up, he said, "We have to go find the boys. Take care. Enjoy your visit." Nodding in the direction of Alex's parents, he led me away.

We were out of earshot, but his grip on me didn't loosen. "Keep walking. I guarantee they're still watching us."

CHAPTER NINETEEN

"I'll keep walking, but you need to keep holding on so I don't fall down. Lot's of things we obviously need to catch up on," I said, looking up at him with a beaming smile.

He slowed enough to kiss me hard on the lips, his grin as big as mine. "I love how you roll with the punches. Thank you, you were perfect."

"The fiancé part came from Runner. That's how *he* introduced me. But you did well yourself, not reacting to the shock when I said it."

"It's not like it would be a detestable thought, right?" He stopped and turned toward me with a crowd of people flowing around us. Taking my face in his hands, he said, "I've never wanted to be married to anyone before, not even Ann when we found out she was pregnant. But everything about it felt right when the words left your lips. No shock involved. Just a sense of rightness."

What was he saying? Now was not the time to talk about it, but the swarm of butterflies that gathered in my stomach was trying to set themselves free.

"And thank you for not reacting when you met Alex," he said, taking my hand, leading the way toward the arcade.

"Well, it might've been good if you'd told me beforehand. You know it opens up dozens of questions."

"First off, *when* would I have told you? You just found out about Runner, and it never occurred to me we'd run into them tonight, trust me," he said with a snicker. "Secondly, it probably would've taken a while for me to build up the nerve to tell you anyway."

"Good grief, why?"

"Because I spent a long time thinking there was something wrong with me, thinking I was less than a man because the woman who I'd been so close to, who gave birth to my son, decided she preferred to have sex with another woman."

"Holy heavens, I hope you've disabused yourself of *that* thought? I've known my share of men, and believe me, you're as good as they come. How long have she and Alex been together?"

"They met when Runner was a baby. That's when Ann realized she didn't want to be a mom, and definitely didn't want to live with a man. She signed all rights over to me when he was six months old. I haven't been civil to her since."

"But she has Rachel." The thought made me want to explode. How can you turn your back on one child and embrace another?

"Rachel is a product of their union. Ann was inseminated by an unknown donor, and they've been a close, quiet family ever since."

"But it's so unfair to Runner!" I said, disgusted.

"He's not suffering, and unless he has to see her, he's fine. It's been good to see what a healthy respect and affection he has for you. He's close to Maggie, and was very close to my mom, but it has been encouraging to find out he can be genuinely fond of a strange woman in my life."

"Strange? Speak for yourself, buddy." We laughed, then I stopped.

"What happened at school the other day? Did it have something to do with his mom? Is that why you took off in such a hurry?"

"Perceptive of you," he said. The boys were playing in the arcade, happy and noisy as they competed on opposing machines, so we stood outside, continuing our conversation.

"No matter how much the school system tries to teach them about sex, I think kids should be allowed to be innocent until they're ready. It's one of the reasons we've stayed in Sugarloaf. That and because, after my mom died, I didn't want to pull him away from the only home he's known. He doesn't live in a bubble, we talk about anything he wants to talk about, and he's obviously always known his mom lives with a woman. He's a pretty street-smart kid, but I never wanted him bombarded with stuff he didn't have to know too soon."

"So what happened?" I asked, watching as Runner beat kid after kid in the ball toss.

"Now he's getting to an age where kids are cruel, no matter where you live. Middle school is like a bear with hemorrhoids, so I've kinda been preparing him for it. I didn't expect to have it so 'in your face' while he's still in elementary."

"Amazing how fast they grow up, isn't it?"

"Heck, yeah. His mom's sexuality has always just been a given in his life. He didn't see her much, he's never been overly fond of her, but we didn't make a big deal of it either. If he wanted to talk about her, we did.

If he had questions, I answered them to the best of my ability."

"Has she ever been close to him?"

"Never," he said. "He was like something out of a bad dream for her, an alien. Although I think it had a lot to do with me, quite frankly."

"What do you mean?"

"Ann and I were good friends. We just kinda drifted into sex. I was her first, and apparently, her only," he laughed. "She didn't enjoy it no matter what I did, and I'm not sure at the time she even understood it herself. But when she met Alex, her world changed, and I think she just associated Runner with my disgusting manhood."

"Yeah, totally disgusting."

"But he never suffered. My mom and Maggie were there, and he's had as much love as it's possible to give one child."

"I can't imagine a more well-adjusted kid. You've done an extraordinary job. Now tell me what happened at school."

Miles' shoulders dropped. "In the natural way kids that age will be, someone made a crude comment about things his mother likes to do. Totally out of character, Runner took a swing at the kid."

"Oh, God," I said.

"Maggie got to the school in a hurry and picked him up. She and my mom have never been able to tolerate Ann. Not because of her lifestyle choice, but because of her non-involvement with her son. The parents of the kid he hit were great, and the kid got in trouble for bullying as well, but the school wanted me to keep Runner home for a few days to let things die down."

"That's why you didn't call."

"Yeah, I took the day off and we spent it together until the afternoon. It was a huge learning experience for both of us, and we had some of the best talks ever. Then Maggie stopped by to bring dinner and find out how things were going, then you showed up."

"Right? Look what the cat dragged in?"

"I'm so glad you did. I'd been thinking of you all afternoon, wanting to call and having absolutely no idea what I was going to say to you. I hate lies and knew I wouldn't be able to come up with a reasonable excuse that you wouldn't see right through. I know what it must've taken for you to show up, but I couldn't have been happier to see anyone."

"Seriously?"

"Seriously. I knew you'd be finding out in a hurry about Runner, and you had said you weren't going back to New York. You and I were far enough along in our relationship that it was time to tell you, and I apologize I didn't get the words out before he got home." We laughed at how it had come about. "You handled it like a trooper, you know. Kinda like tonight. I watched your face both nights, and no one would've known the explosion that had just detonated before your eyes." He squeezed me against him.

"You've got to admit it's been an interesting few days. And you were worried I was leaving the excitement behind in New York." I rose on tiptoes to kiss his cheek, but his lips met mine instead.

"I can't even find words to tell you what you mean to me," he said, running a thumb across my cheek.

"The look in your eyes will suffice for now. Let's get the boys."

We watched a puppet show, had balloons made, bought pirate hats and swords in the gift shop, and ate sopapillas with honey until we were stuffed. It had been a long but wonderful day, and I'd taken a lot of pictures. As we left the restaurant, Runner took my hand and asked his dad if he would take a picture of us in front of the fountain.

"Sure thing," he said, getting his phone out to snap some shots. I stood on the ground and Runner stood on the edge of the fountain, his hand on my shoulder, towering over me, a huge smile on his face. Then he and James Gabriel drew their swords and had a mock battle while we shot photos.

In the car on the way home, I felt the elusive happiness I'd been seeking. How could I have possibly imagined even a month ago this is what my life would look like today? It was still in the developing stages, but I was good with where it was going. James Gabriel talked non-stop for the first half-hour on the way home, then the yawns took over as he curled up against the door. Runner leaned forward and squeezed my shoulder. "Thanks for having my back in there," he said quietly.

I turned in my seat to look at him. There was a fine line I was walking here. I knew Miles didn't have women in Runner's life because he didn't want them leaving, and I wasn't about to presume I was going to be a permanent fixture, but I loved this kid, and I would demolish anyone to protect him.

"I don't know if you know the habits of Mama Bears," I said, holding his hand, "but I have a lot of those instincts for people I love." I wasn't going to explain that because I didn't want to come on too strong, but he could filter it as he wanted or needed.

"Mama Bears are tough and aggressive, and will go to extreme lengths to protect what's theirs. If it's in my power, I'll never let anyone hurt you, no matter who they are. So no thanks are necessary, just doing what comes naturally." I pursed my lips and gave his hand a squeeze as encouragement. He didn't let go of my hand until we pulled in front of James Gabriel's house.

When we arrived in front of Madeline Manor, Runner and I shared a smile. "My dad says you're a great cook. Maybe you can come over sometime."

"I'd like that a lot. Thanks for one of the best days I've ever had."

"Me, too."

Miles opened my car door, then walked me to the house. "I'm not going to kiss you the way I want because little eyes are watching, but he's going camping next weekend with Rusty's family. Want to plan on spending that time together?"

"I almost swooned as those words came out of your mouth. Oh, God, the possibilities," I said, head tilting back slightly, eyes partially closed. "Everything about today was perfect – all of it. Kiss me innocently and I promise not to moan and touch you inappropriately. But you better be ready for next weekend." He kissed me chastely. I stood outside until they'd driven away.

My creativity was soaring, and we continued to get new clients. Our little firm continued to flourish, and I went with Callie and Jordan to spend an entire day in Denver and Boulder checking out offices in some of Jack's buildings. We each had jobs that were easy to cover from remote locations, but we'd talked many times of giving our businesses a brick and mortar building, even if we just shared a suite with three offices and a reception area. Not one of us wanted to work full time again, and this seemed a solution that would work for us all.

Miles came every day after work to check on Nana, and twice during the week I went to his house to fix dinner for him and Runner. One night, Runner and I played Scrabble while Miles cleaned up the kitchen and did some things around the house. Maggie came over after she'd put Harper down for the night, both times on the guise of having to pick something up, and ended up staying for hours. She shared stories about the time their mother was dying. Maggie was on bed rest during the last few months of her pregnancy because she'd lost several babies between Caleb and Harper so she needed to be off her feet as much as possible.

Miles and Runner had lived nearby, but when his mom got sick, he set up one of the main-floor bedrooms for her, and what was now his office he set up for Maggie. Luke dropped Maggie and Caleb off every day so Miles could not only take care of mom, but Maggie as well. For Maggie's sake, she was also able to spend time with their mother, even though she couldn't take care of any of her needs. Many days she ended up staying the night.

During that time, Miles rented out his other house and took one of the downstairs rooms here for himself. In the larger room he built a fort for the boys who often spent the night together. From the ceiling he hung two canoes, low to the ground, one on each side of the room, and put mattresses in them for the boys to sleep. He painted the wood floors blue to give the illusion of a tranquil lake, and had trees cut in half and attached to the walls. It actually felt like being outdoors, and was one of the coolest rooms I'd ever seen.

Harper was born a few weeks before their mother died, but Maggie and her family stayed often because they knew there wasn't much time left. Hospice helped out the last week. After mom passed, Maggie told me Miles threw himself into his work, not only to make up for the lost time Jack had let him take off, but because it had been so much harder on him than he'd expected. The stories she shared gave me deeper insight into the man that had captured my heart.

CHAPTER TWENTY

The week came and went. My excitement over the upcoming weekend grew to a point where I was ready to burst with it. I'd been thinking of being with Miles, and while we have total privacy at the Manor, I had other ideas in mind. I spent a good part of the afternoon checking the clock, planning and getting everything ready. Tonight was going to be an experience unlike any either of us had ever had. I had prepared a meal, and had the wine and all of the utensils packed in Jordan's unique picnic basket. I had taken great care in getting ready, and had changed my clothes at least three times. Wanting this to be an unforgettable night, when Miles arrived after the end of a long work day, I had him shower in The Library before our adventure began. He'd brought a small overnight case, and just the thought of that sent my senses into overdrive.

I hadn't seen Jordan in a few hours, so I texted to let her know Miles and I were going out for dinner and not to lock the back door. I intended for us to be home at some point before morning. When he was dressed, I picked up a large quilt from the linen closet. "You get to drive, sir. We're not going far."

"As you wish," he said, offering me his arm to escort me to the car. I'd found a back way to get to the sanctuary in the pines, and it wouldn't take more than a minute to walk to our destination after we parked the car. Leading him the short distance, I had him close his eyes the last few feet. I was pretty impressed with how everything had turned out, and I couldn't wait to see his reaction.

The picnic table had a white linen tablecloth covering it that was attached with straps. The table was set with fresh flowers, crystal and china, and dimly lit lanterns emanated a feeling of romance. I had blown up a queen-sized air mattress and set it nearby, covered in Egyptian cotton sheets. The weight of the picnic basket held it in place in case of an errant wind while I was gone. A few feet from each corner stood more lanterns, giving just enough light to cast a romantically eerie glow halfway up the trees. It was even more spectacular walking into it as the sun was setting and the light from the lanterns was picking up the bulk of the duty. It was more beautiful than I could have hoped for.

I set the large quilt on the mattress and brought the picnic basket to the table. Miles stood with a dazed expression on his rugged face, taking in the splendor of this unbroken emerald forest. Limbs of the trees meshed overhead, and flames barely flickered because of the density of the leaves. "How did you ever find this?"

"It's where I brought Nana the other day. Jordan told me she and Brandan had found a clearing where they have picnics, and Brandan built the table with the benches attached. I've come to think of it as Cathedral Pines. I wanted something special for us tonight, and I kept envisioning this place. What do you think?"

"I can't think. It's extraordinary. I can't believe you did all this," he said with a fair degree of reverence in his voice.

"I've been looking forward to tonight, and had a long time to think about it. I've never made love outdoors, but I still like my creature comforts," I said, pointing to the bed. "I figured if I was going to do something this outrageous, there's no one else I'd rather do it with than you, and I couldn't think of anywhere else I'd rather be than here." I curled my arms around his waist and up his back under his jacket.

The smell of leather and pine surrounded me as his lips met mine tenderly. "Where shall we eat first?" I asked seductively.

"If we don't sit at the table and feast on the banquet you brought, I'm afraid all of your grand efforts will go to waste. What's on the menu?"

"Let's see," I said, pulling out containers. "Potato salad with bacon and barbeque sauce. Sounds weird but totally delicious. Curried chicken with apples, grapes, and pecans in a homemade bread roll, deviled eggs, milk chocolate cookies with malted marshmallow-cream filling, wine."

"How in the world do you stay so small when you cook like that?"

"Like I have time to cook in my real life." I sat next to him. The rustling leaves set the tone for the gentleness of our conversation. "So tell me about Ann," I asked quietly.

"Ah, Ann," he said with a smile. "It was like being hit by a truck, then realizing when the truck moves off you how much better it feels. It took me a long time to get back on my feet after she and Alex hooked up. Not only had my son, whom I loved more than life itself, lost his mother, I'd lost my best friend. The problem with being involved with someone who's gay is that there's no way to fight it. It's like crashing into a brick wall."

"That makes total sense. And the shock of it must've been devastating."

"We'd lived together, talked about our future with this young human we'd made, and then, overnight, everything we'd known was gone. I'd lost my friend, my companion. It was a paradigm shift. It's natural to wonder what you did wrong, and you start to question everything from your judgment to your manhood."

My eyes widened as I leaned over to take his hand. "You know it had absolutely nothing to do with you, right?"

"I know that now." He got a slight grin on his face when he looked at me. "I kept wondering if I could've kept her if I'd been better in bed."

I nearly choked on the bite I'd put in my mouth. "It's not possible to be better in bed."

"After a while I found my balance. Wouldn't have traded it for the world because I got Runner; glad it turned out the way it did because, after you showed up, I understood why nothing else had ever worked."

He just threw that out there? Our eyes devoured each other, his words stirring hidden pulses. "That was one of the nicest things you've ever said to me. You tryin' to get laid, buddy?"

In a voice as smooth as chocolate, he said, "That would be a nice conclusion to an already perfect evening."

We put the food and dishes in the cooler and basket. He wrapped me in his arms and whispered in my ear, "May I have this dance?"

Swaying to the music only we could hear, accompanied by the murmur and laugh of a gypsy wind, he lowered his head and ran his tongue across the sensitive hollow of my neck. "After she left, I tried to prove to myself that I was desirable," he said quietly. "For a few months, I went through a lot of women." He pulled his head away far enough to see my expression.

"Am I supposed to react to that?" I asked. "I probably would've, too. Well, men, not women."

"I learned a lot from that particular period, too," he continued. "I learned quickly it wasn't at all who I am, and I'd started to loathe myself. I needed to be proud of me to be a good dad to Runner."

"You succeeded brilliantly."

He pulled me closer again. "I came to grips with the incomprehensible whims of fate, knowing that neither of us could've ever changed who we were, together or apart. And I learned that it's the relationship, not the mechanics, that makes the sex good or not."

We stopped swaying. With eyes that burned, he touched my hair, drawing me like the moon draws water. My spirit wrapped around him as I felt my heart dissolve to my toes. Tender, not the uncontrolled white-hot passion we knew, but not any less exciting.

He lifted my shirt over my head and let my bra fall to the ground. His eyes worshipped my body, appearing to savor the vision as his hands gently cupped my breasts. I slipped my pants off, and stood in the darkness before him, the light from the lanterns licking the rounded curves of my body and my pebbled nipples.

He lifted one of my arms. His lips caressed my wrist. My hand curled into his hair as his tongue found the sensitive flesh inside my elbow. "Lie down," he whispered, his voice rippling with seductive intent, slowly removing his own clothes, never breaking eye contact as I lay on the silky sheets, not able to see all of him in the shadows. I'd never been more turned on.

His knee tested the edge of the mattress to see how much bouncing there'd be, and a slow smile crossed his face just before it disappeared to nuzzle the inside of my thigh. I cried out in pleasure as his tongue found my most sensitive nerve cluster.

"I stop thinking when I touch you." His voice was hoarse, we were suspended in time. "You can cry out all you want and no one will hear you. God, just the thought of that is a rush." His tongue knew just where to move, and as his finger inside me pulled toward his mouth, my need exploded in waves and spasms that had me shattering in pleasure. His tongue slowed, and he placed gentle kisses on my heightened sensitivity before kissing my navel, my breasts, my neck. His hardness taunted my opening as his lips took mine.

"It's such a turn-on to taste me on your lips," I whispered. His embrace deepened as our hips moved against each other, teasing me, covering him with my moistness. With one hard, deep thrust, he was inside me, stilling, allowing my body to get used to his size, his mouth drawing a desperate duel with mine. I ran my fingernails down his back, wanting him harder, aching for him.

He obliged with faster, deeper plunges, making sure he was pressing against my exceptionally sensitive bud as my muscles squeezed around him. As my orgasm started to release, my thighs gripped his hips to pull him in to penetrate as intensely as possible. I moaned because it was earth shattering in its force as we reached our climax within seconds of each other.

As our breathing quieted, he stroked each of my eyes with his lips, then captured my mouth again in a gentle stilling of what had just happened between us. "I love you," he murmured. My heart sang itself to sleep.

The thunder had been no more than a distant rumbling as we slumbered in each other's arms. The rain woke us both as it started. Gentle at first, raindrops the size of bullets thundered through the thick foliage, and I was concerned how much harder it must be on the other side of the solid canopy of leaves. "Hurry, get your clothes on," Miles said, jumping from the mattress. We were both dressed in seconds, and he began breaking down the bed as I packed the picnic basket and collected lanterns.

"You can set those under the table for tonight," he said, his voice getting louder to be heard above the pellets of rain and wind. "We'll come back for them tomorrow, but they'll be protected if the storm gets too heavy in here."

When everything was gathered at the table, Miles said loudly, "Can you carry the basket and the blanket? I'll carry the mattress partially deflated to hold over us until we make it to the truck. I have a feeling it's a lot harder where we're going than it is in here."

Taking as much as we could in one trip and making sure everything else was protected, we made a run for it. It took a lot longer to get to the car than it had taken to get from the car. Lightning crackled around us like the recoil of a whip, and rain poured in buckets. We put everything in the back seat and leapt into the front, closing the doors against a torrential downpour. We were soaked.

Both of us gasping, it took a few moments for our breathing to calm. "Well, wasn't that fun?" I asked with no small degree of irony. "We'll have to do that again sometime."

He took my chin in his cold hand, water dripping from his eyelashes and the end of his nose. "Listen to me. That was one of the most incredible experiences of my life. No matter how it ended, nothing will ever take away from the perfection of what happened between us out there. You planned the perfect interlude, we *had* the perfect interlude. It doesn't get better than it was."

I kissed the palm of his damp hand. Drenched, we were satisfied to let the heater work its magic to cut through the layer of chill that held us immobile. "Can't go anywhere until the defroster catches up, and I imagine it will take a few minutes because of the humidity in here."

"Let's make a deal. Next time we have sex outside, let's at least find our way inside before we fall asleep. "

"Deal," he said, kissing me before he started fiddling to put the defroster on its highest speed, and turning the windshield wipers on at a steady pace. Rivulets dripped down my neck, but I was so cold I barely noticed.

Coming in the back door, he hung his wet jacket that glistened like seals' fur. The storm was raging by the time we had everything put away, and lightning illuminated the darkness as we walked from the kitchen to The Library. "I checked with Rusty's dad.

They holed up in Greeley at a Fairfield Inn. The boys didn't mind because it has a pool, so all is well."

Hail started pounding the south side of the house, sounding as though we'd been caught in the crosshairs of a machine gun fight. "Thank God we made it back in time. There'll be flooding with this one." Changing into dry clothes, we went to the main living area.

"Oh! I'm so glad you're home!" Jordan said. Brandan was at the porch window watching the flying debris and destruction of the leaves. Miles stood next to him as we watched raindrops pattern the window.

"Have you ever seen anything like it?"

"Nope. I imagine it's striking dread in nature herself," Miles said quietly. "There'll be millions in damage, at least. So many people in town still live in the shacks their grandparents built decades ago and don't have insurance. What a mess."

Like a brittle explosion, we heard the sound of glass breaking on the second floor, and Miles and Brandan took the stairs two at a time. Brandan came back just as quickly and headed to the basement. "Window in the laundry caught a falling limb. I've got some plywood, we can board it up for the night."

A few minutes later as Brandan headed back up the stairs, the house suddenly became ominously dark and quiet.

"Hey, Jordan," he called, "would you mind grabbing some of the lanterns so we can finish getting this covered? Miles is holding a shower curtain over it to keep some of the rain out."

"On my way!" she said as we both hurried down the stairs.

"I'm so glad you have lots of these," I said as we each pulled a couple from the shelf. "I left four of them under the picnic table as the storm started, and I'd feel awful if there weren't a bunch more."

"So *that's* where you guys went, huh? I knew you had something special planned. Did you have fun?"

"Fun doesn't being to describe it," I said, pretending like I was fanning myself as we both laughed. "I put the lighter back in the kitchen, so we can grab it on our way through."

I could hear my phone ringing from The Library. "I'll be right there, here's the lighter." Who in the world was calling at this hour?

CHAPTER TWENTY-ONE

They were finishing the window repair while Jordan put several more towels down to soak up some of the water. "It's Nana, she's gone," I said, breathless. "That was Miriam. The electricity went down and she went to check on Nana and she wasn't in bed. She tried to call us, but the intercom wasn't working without electricity. What are we going to do?" I was torn between being hysterical that she might be out in the elements, or that she was safely in the kitchen.

"The kitchen!" I said, racing off. The others were close on my heels, each with a lantern, but there was no sign of Nana. "We'll check the basement," Miles said. Jordan pulled a few flashlights out of a cabinet and handed one to me.

"This is a little easier to maneuver." We joined them and looked at every square inch. I even called several times to her, but to no avail. "Would she really have gone out in this?" I asked, a sense of panic beginning to overtake me.

"I'll go look for her," Miles said. "I've got my Jeep."

"I'm coming with you," I said.

"No, I need you to stay right here with Jordan," Brandan said. "I'll go with Miles, and we'll keep our phones on so we can all stay in communication."

"She won't survive if she's out in this." I couldn't even imagine.

"They'll find her, don't you worry. Let's get the laundry room cleaned up while they're gone. It'll give us something to do."

We gave them high-powered flashlights and blankets in case they found her. They both put on heavy parkas, Miles hugged me, then ran to the car. "Make sure your phones are on," Brandan said, kissing Jordan as Miles pulled the Jeep as close as he could to the back door.

We were using our phones like walkie-talkies, but after a half hour I was frustrated not being able to help. "I'm going to the cottage," I said. The hail had stopped, but it continued to be a torrential downpour.

"Why on earth would you do that?" Jordan asked.

"She's getting out somehow. There's something we're missing. I want to look around. Hell, what I really want is something to occupy me besides waiting."

"I'm coming with you," Jordan said, getting us both windbreakers. "No sense taking umbrellas, they'd be destroyed by the wind within ten feet. Call Miriam, tell her we're coming. Make sure the door is unlocked."

There were at least three or four inches of hail piled against the back door when we opened it. "Are we really gonna do this?" Jordan asked.

"Of course we are. It's us, silly. Ready?"

We did a lightning zigzag run at double speed and were to the cottage in under a minute, but we were cold and drenched as we stepped inside. Miriam was beside herself, but I would never blame her for what happened, none of us could figure it out. "We just want to check around, see if there's something we've all overlooked in the past."

"Believe me, I've spent the last half hour tearing the place apart. I can't figure it out."

"Jordan and I are pretty good sleuths. If there's something here, we'll find it." Nana was fascinated with the grandfather clock, and I scrutinized it for several minutes. She was always polishing the glass and talking to Henry in it. I opened the door, but there was nothing at all that would give us a clue.

Fifteen minutes later we were scratching our heads. I called Miles for an update, and things didn't look good. It was still lightning and pouring, the storm system seeming to have stalled over the town. He and Brandan were battered and at a loss where else to look. "We've been to the reservoir, drove around as much of it as we could. Went by the Amber Rose, all the places she might have gone, but it makes it doubly difficult with all the lights in town off. We even drove by James Gabriel's house, but their lights are off, too."

"What are we gonna do?" I asked with a catch in my throat.

"We're gonna keep looking. We're alternating each stop which of us gets out. We'll find her."

I kept thinking about where else they could look, and thought about all the times I'd looked and she and James Gabriel had appeared to be sharing a secret. He often sat adoringly at her feet. Was it possible he might know something?

"April, I'm so sorry to bother you. I know it's two o'clock in the morning, but can I talk to James Gabriel? Nana's been missing for over an hour, and I was hoping against hope he might know something."

"Sure you can talk to him. No one's sleeping around here. The fans turned off with the electric outage, the nightlights went off, we have candles burning, but no way the boys are going to sleep. Let me get him for you."

"Hello?" a sleepy young voice said.

"Hi, James Gabriel, it's Jeni. Listen, I know you and Nana share a lot of secrets, and I wouldn't ever want you to tell a secret that somebody's asked you to keep, but this is very important. Nana's missing, and I wondered if you might know where she is?"

"Maybe," he said, hesitantly.

"The storm's awfully bad, and she won't be able to survive long if she's caught out there."

"But I promised," he said. I could hear April talking to him very sweetly, telling him how proud she was that he was so faithful to keep a secret, but Nana might die if he didn't tell us, and he wouldn't want that, would he?

"No, ma'am."

"Then tell Jeni where you think Nana is so she can help rescue her."

"Well, she's not in any danger. She's safe."

"Please tell me, sweetheart. Brandan and Miles are out looking for her. You don't want them to be hurt, do you?" I was sure he was thinking of his dad, and how Brandan had almost died trying to rescue his father, and I wasn't above pushing a little harder. "Remember how much you love Brandan? It would be so sad for all of us if something happened to him, wouldn't it?"

After a long pause, James Gabriel let out a heavy sigh. "I can't tell you, I'll have to show you." I hated that he sounded defeated, but I didn't know any other way.

"Oh, honey, have your mom get a coat on you. The rain seems to be letting up a little. Brandan and Miles will be there in just a few minutes to get you, okay?"

"Okay."

"You're doing a wonderful thing. I promise you it's okay, and Nana won't be mad. Hold tight and the guys will be right there."

Jordan had called Brandan from her phone, and they were knocking on his door while he and I were talking. "It's gonna be all right, James Gabriel," I said as I hung up the phone.

"Ask Brandan where they're going," I said to Jordan, who was still on the phone. "Not sure where James Gabriel is taking them."

"They're coming here to the cottage."

"You've got to be kidding!"

They were here within minutes. As they walked in, James Gabriel looked at Brandan and said, "You promise I'm not gonna get in trouble?"

"Not only are you not gonna get in trouble," Brandan said, "I'm gonna give you twenty dollars for being so brave."

"*Really?* Twenty *whole* dollars?" he said in excitement.

"Twenty whole dollars," Brandan agreed, taking it out of his wallet.

James Gabriel made a beeline to the grandfather clock set in an alcove next to the fireplace. He looked back at us with a sense of resignation and placed his hand around a knob on the base of the right column, then twisted to the left. Goosebumps covered my arms as the body of the clock moved silently into the space behind the chimney. The frame remained intact around the opening where the clock had been, and it would have been impossible for any of us to have ever noticed there were separate pieces.

Coming to a stop about two feet behind where it had been sitting just moments before, there was a collective gasp as James Gabriel smiled a mischievous smile and disappeared down a narrow flight of stairs.

Brandan and Jordan gave each other a questioning look. "Willow?" they said in unison. Having no idea what they were talking about, Miles and I turned on our flashlights to illuminate the black hole into which he had vanished. It took merely moments for all of us to follow him into a tunnel that seemed to reach into the never-ending darkness. It was tall enough for both Brandan and Miles to stand to their full heights, and I couldn't begin to imagine who'd excavated it or why.

Already far ahead, we followed what appeared to be candlelight. No one spoke as Brandan led our little entourage past wood beams that continued as far as the eye could see. We rushed ahead, getting closer, but the light no longer seemed as direct. Taking a sudden left turn, we stopped abruptly when we found James Gabriel sitting on the floor next to Nana, holding her hand as she sat calmly in an antique rocker. Appearing dazed, she looked at each of us.

"Did the house fall down?" she asked.

"No, the storm has passed and it's all quiet again," I said, kneeling on one knee on the other side of her.

Miles touched my shoulder and said quietly, "Brandan and I will be right back. Take her to the cottage when she's ready." I nodded in understanding.

"Wanna go home now?" I asked, looking at the side tunnel where we found ourselves. It ended abruptly about fifteen feet deep from the main access. In addition to the rocker, there was a smaller chair and two wooden chests with a lantern standing between them.

When she didn't respond, Jordan walked past us and opened the lid to one of the chests. With a small gasp, she fell to her knees, reached in and reverently withdrew a journal. Reading the first page, she closed the journal softly. She pulled out four more while I continued to shine the light on them for her to read. She set each one tenderly back in the box. Obviously moved with emotion, she said, "They're Willow's journals."

"That's amazing." Smiling, I said, "Who's Willow?"

She closed the lid. "She was the daughter of Edward and Jordan Stratton, the couple who built Madeline Manor. According to records Brandan and I discovered when we renovated the main house, Willow was born in 1894. I'm shaking I'm so excited."

"Talk about right up your alley!" I said. "I can't imagine anything more exciting for someone who likes research as much as you do to find something like that!"

"Right?"

Nana continued to rock with James Gabriel next to her. Indicating with a nod that Jordan wanted me to shine the light on the other trunk, she carefully lifted the unlocked lid. Leaning over her shoulder, the light reflected off metals. Missing spoons from the Manor, the candlesticks, salt and pepper shakers, and several things I had no idea were missing. They sat on a bed of – "What is that?" I asked in awe.

"Gold," Jordan said reverently.

"How can you be so sure?" I asked, half teasing, not wanting to touch but not being able to take my eyes off it.

"I'll tell you later." She shook her head and closed the lid softly. "Let's get Nana back to the cottage." I couldn't believe how calm she was being.

Jordan and I helped Nana to her feet. "Why did you put the silver in there, Nana?"

Not sure if she would understand what I was asking, it was surprising when she said, "Because that's where they keep the valuables."

Okay, on one level that made sense. Holding the flashlight as James Gabriel held Nana's hand, we led her back to the ladder from where we'd come. We could hear voices in the tunnel as we got back to the living room, and left the shaft open for Brandan and Miles. Electricity was on again, and the winds and rain had died down.

"Absolutely, positively ingenious," Miles said as James Gabriel closed the clock entrance behind them. "When you get to the other side, it opens into the basement of the Manor. But when the door is closed over there, no one would be able to tell there's even a door. It's built into a panel of wainscoting, and the lines all blend together. It's like a century-old panic room. Who the hell do you think built it?"

Jordan and Brandan looked at each other. "It's still the middle of the night," I said. "April is probably pacing the floors. Let's get James Gabriel home, and we can talk about this later."

"Yes, you guys go on," Miriam said, seemingly stunned. "I'm so glad that problem is solved. I was beginning to think I'd lost my mind. Thank you so much. I can get her to bed from here."

The headlights illuminated green streets from leaves that covered them from the destructive storm, and there were inches of hail on the sides of the road. Four of us were silent only momentarily after we dropped James Gabriel off and headed back to the Manor, then everyone started talking at once. We were all excited to share our stories, and Brandan was the one who started as we jumped over puddles to make it into the kitchen.

"I didn't want to say anything in front of anyone else because the fewer people who know what I'm going to tell you, the better," he began. "When we started work on the renovations of this place, Jordan found a secret room on the third floor." Miles and I showed an appropriate amount of surprise and shock and excitement.

Brandan continued. "It's accessed by a unique mechanism in a bookshelf in Willow's Nest."

"Can't wait to examine that," Miles said. "Go on."

"The intricacy of the tunnel and access to and from both ends appears to have been made by the same person who did the secret room upstairs. It's mind-blowing."

"When Brandan was in a coma," Jordan continued, "I found a hiding place inside the secret room." Pausing for effect, she looked at Miles, then me, then took a deep breath. "I don't need to tell you all of the ramifications if word of this leaks out, but we found," another deep breath, "gold – lots of it."

"*What?*" Miles and I said in unison.

"You're serious?" Miles asked, looking at Brandan.

"Yep," he took over the story. "Jordan and I couldn't spend all of it in three lifetimes, so we've been trying to figure out what to do with some of it."

"Before you go any further," Jordan said, looking between the men, "there's something I need to tell you."

"Yes?" Brandan said in a way that made it two syllables. "We're waiting."

"In the alcove where we found Nana, there were two more chests," she said excitedly. "Even more exciting than one of them being half full of gold, the other had several of Willow's journals."

"Did you bring them out?"

"No, I was in such a state of shock over everything going on, I figured they'd last another few days down there. I didn't want to run the risk of bringing them into the open and possibly having them get wet. And we didn't know yet where the tunnel led, or if it led anywhere."

"Speaking of which," Miles said, "you have to see where it *does* lead. Absolutely, positively, friggin' genius."

CHAPTER TWENTY-TWO

We headed to the basement and Miles and Brandan showed us the wall with the door that led to the tunnel. Even knowing it was there, it took Jordan and I almost ten minutes to find the actual opening. "Has to be the same guy," Jordan said, examining the hinges. "What in the world do you suppose it was for, and who could've built it?"

"Hopefully the journals will again reveal the mysteries," Brandan said in a sardonic tone of voice.

"It's four o'clock in the morning," I said, stifling a yawn. "The sun will be coming up soon. Let's talk about all this fascinating stuff after we catch a few hours of sleep."

The house was still dark as we parted ways in the living room. As Jordan and Brandan headed up the stairs, I said, "I'll never be able to thank you enough for risking your lives to find Nana. From start to finish, it's been a memorable day."

I took Miles' hand as we walked to The Library. "Thank you for making my decision to move here so easy. I would've come for Nana, but you've made it so much more enjoyable."

Several hours later we woke in each other's arms. "Do we have anything specific on the agenda today?" he asked.

"Not that I know of. Do you have something in mind?"

"I can't wait to take a look at the tunnel when we're not on a mission, but I'd like to run by my house and Maggie's house and see what kind of damage was done."

"I'd love to do that!"

Buckling our seat belts, he kissed me as though we hadn't just had toe-curling sex. "Best thunder storm ever," he said with a twinkle of amusement. "It'll be impossible to forget."

We stopped by Maggie's first. The street appeared as though a child had been let loose with a box of green crayons, melted and scattered haphazardly. She fixed lunch while I played with Harper, and there was, blessedly, no damage but a few chips of missing paint to a porch railing. It was early afternoon when we got to his house and walked around to see if there was exterior damage. In the side yard was enough wood, quartered and neatly stacked, to last several seasons if you burned it every day.

"Why do you have so much firewood?"

"Up here, a man's wealth isn't measured by the kind of car he drives, but by the amount of firewood he has," he said, only half teasing. "I had a lot of hours and a lot of frustration when my mom was sleeping. This was a good way to let off steam." As we came in through the garage door, he said, "If you want lemonade, there's always some fresh in the 'fridge."

"I'll get it," I offered. "Do you want some?"

"Yeah, I'll be right back."

When I turned, he was leaning in the doorway with what appeared to be a letter, no movement, his eyes not leaving me, as though he were weighing a decision.

"Is something wrong?" I asked, concerned.

He approached without saying a word and handed me the letter.

Dear Dad,

You asked me to give you an answer when I get home on Sunday night, but there's no need for me to wait that long because there was never really a question.

You want to know how I'd feel about you marrying Jeni?

Miles had gone back to the doorway, arms crossed, watching me.

You've never really struck me as dumb, but the first thing I'd say is, "What took you so long?" You're not getting any younger, and neither am I. You need her, and I really like her. Seriously, I'd even say I'd like having her around all the time. Heck, even Rusty likes her, and that's saying a lot.

So get it taken care of. Rather than giving you my answer when I come home, I want you to give me her answer. Don't screw it up, k? Better not be anything but 'yes.' Got that? Glad you're my dad, Runner

We didn't move, hardly breathed, just stared. "Is this a proposal?"

"You gonna say 'yes'?"

I wanted to drag this feeling out for a few minutes, wanted to be conscious of the rush in every cell in my body. When I saw the look on his face, it made me sad for him that he wasn't sure of my answer.

"I'm a pretty busy woman," I said sassily. "If we can get this done in the next two weeks, consider it a deal.

If not, I'll have to figure out when I can work you into my schedule."

His shoulders relaxed as he stood away from the wall and opened his arms. I was in them before I'd taken my next breath. "Yes, yes, yes, yes, yes," I said, placing kisses all over his gorgeous face. "I want to be a huge part of your world. I want to be the tail to your kite that brings you balance and makes you soar."

What followed was slow, sweet, heart-stopping lovemaking. We did a few things around the house, but couldn't seem to stop touching, stop kissing. An hour later we found ourselves wrapped in each other's arms on his huge bed, both of us exhausted. I'm not sure how long we'd been dozing when Miles suddenly jumped from the bed.

"Come on," he said, a wide grin on his face. "The kite tail gave me a great idea."

He went to a hall closet and pulled out a white sheet. "Would you please cut this the long way, about three feet wide?"

"Seriously?"

"Yep. I'll be right back."

"Perfect," he said as he took the torn sheet and spread it on the grass in the back yard. "We'll put this across the front of the house so Runner can see it when he gets home tomorrow afternoon." A few minutes later, he put his arm around me and kissed me hard as we stood back to admire his homemade banner that proclaimed, "She said YES!"

EPILOGUE

Seven years later

The crowd that gathered today at Madeline Manor was nothing like the intimate gathering of close friends and family who came together to celebrate our wedding in Cathedral Pines two weeks after Runner arrived home to find his father's banner. Flowers that loved the shade had blanketed the ground as our decorations, and Jordan had loaned me a vintage, white-lace dress that belonged to one of her ancestors. It had been perfect for the occasion. Nana had been growing frailer, but there were several times that day I felt she was actually aware of what was happening.

Today's company was overflowing the Manor and spilling onto the lush lawns that surrounded it. They were gathered to celebrate the high school graduation of Runner and some of his friends. The boy I'd met all those years ago had grown into a young man that anyone would be proud of. He received scholarship offers from around the country. In the end he opted to take the offer from University of Northern Colorado, not too far away in Greeley. He told me often he didn't want his little sister, Elizabeth, to grow up not knowing who he was, and it was the only school in Colorado that offered baseball opportunities. He was excited to be close enough to be able to drive his new Jeep home when he had the chance.

"Mind if I join you?" Jordan asked, stepping onto the porch.

"I'd love that." I patted the wicker rocker next to me.

"Thinking about anything in particular, or just escaping the crowd for a while?"

"Actually feeling faintly overwhelmed with emotion right now. Looking at these beautiful children we've created and raised. Thinking of how proud my mom and Nana would be to see the legacy they left. Looking at the future leaders out there, some still in diapers, and thinking what an awesome responsibility it is. No, I'm not thinking about anything in particular," I laughed.

"Sometimes I look back on our college days and wonder if there was any way we could've imagined this would be our future. All the things we thought we wanted pale in comparison to what we actually got."

"And I think about the little twists in fate that got us here. What if Andrew hadn't been such a dick and cheated on you? What if Riley hadn't had a heart attack and I'd gone back to New York? How *is* he, by the way?"

"Ornery as ever," she laughed. "He and mom will be out next month. They want to be here for Edward's fifth birthday. Dear Lord, they spoil that child. Can't imagine what he'll get *this* year."

"You know *I* certainly don't mind the gifts they send. They get handed down to Elizabeth, she gets the best of the best, Edward is her hero for 'sharing' his toys so well – *after* he's outgrown them, of course. Yep, perfect set up."

Jordan took my hand as we rocked and watched the kids playing in the field, watched Runner showing James Gabriel and the younger boys for the umpteenth time how to hold the ball properly, then giving them each a chance to try it themselves. "I know he was already a remarkable kid when you married Miles, but I hope Edward grows up to be anywhere near as admirable as Runner. You've done a superb job with him."

"Thanks, but I don't take a lot of credit for that. Miles gave him such a solid foundation, I just had a lot of fun nurturing it. And I think young Edward there has a lot of Riley in him, so your big challenge is gonna be to cultivate his Brandan side." We laughed.

"I keep thinking of how big Runner's heart is," Jordan said. "How many other kids do you know, when asked what they would do if they came into a large sum of money, their first response would be to help the people in town whose houses had been hurt by the storm? I think about that so often."

"And how generous of you and Brandan to take the money from the passageway to set up a fund for that. It'll last for *our* lifetime, and probably more, when people need it. No one ever has to worry about losing their home, thanks to you two. The whole town benefited. Think about how proud the original Edward would've been of his legacy."

Jack and Callie showed up late. Jack stopped to talk to Miles and Brandan and a group of fathers who'd gathered near the barbeque pit. Charlotte Rose, taller and more mature than other girls her age, found a spot near Runner to watch the festivities. She hero-worshipped him, and had followed him around since she was a little girl.

"Sorry we're late," Callie said, joining us on the porch. "Johnny wanted to get something special for Runner, and we had to pick it up in Denver. Traffic was awful."

"Talk about a kid with a big heart. Johnny's something else. Never saw a kid that shares like he does. Jordan and I were just talking about what a good job we're doing as parents," I laughed, raising my glass of lemonade in salute.

"Isn't that the truth? Jack and I talked on the way back about the *Runner's Renovation Foundation.* Charlotte Rose, of course, had a lot to say about his virtues."

"Remember how he wanted to call it, '*The Hail, Yes! Fund*?" We all laughed as we remembered his enthusiasm.

"Wait a minute!" Jordan exclaimed. "Where in the world did you get that dazzling emerald?" Both she and Callie took my hand to examine it. "How did you keep *that* little gem a secret?"

Rays of sunlight glinted off facets as I held up my hand to look at it for the hundredth time that day. "I know we could debate this 'til the cows come home, but I'm married to the best husband ever created." I could hear the arguments coming, so I held up my hand.

"He gave it to me this morning before we got out of bed."

"Wait, are you blushing?" Callie asked.

"Am I? I was just thinking about this morning." Maybe I was blushing. "Anyway, he said he saw it and it reminded him of my eyes, and he wanted to give me something to thank me for loving Runner all these years as though he were my own child. Like that was a chore, right?"

The conversation continued to swirl — about rings, about which of us had the best husband, about what a good job we were doing, and about how much we loved this little town on the water. Sitting on the front porch of the Madeline Manor that day, I couldn't help but think of our ancestors together, beaming with pride at the legacy they had left behind.

~ THE END ~

If you enjoyed the story of Jeni and Miles, or any of the other books by Mimi Foster, please consider leaving a review. Here's a sneak peek at *Thunder Struck*.

Now an excerpt from...

THUNDER STRUCK

Book 2 in the

Thunder on the Mountain

Series

CHAPTER ONE

As Andrew took my face in his hands and kissed me on the forehead, nose, and lips, there was no way I could have known that my whole world would be turned upside down by this time tomorrow. "So I'll see you for lunch?" he asked.

"That works for me. I have a dress fitting and a few errands in the morning, but I can meet you at The James by noon."

"You sure you won't stay the night? I promise I'll make it worth your while."

"Three more weeks, then we have the rest of our lives. And I have to admit, I'm enjoying our new playfulness. How are you holding up?"

"Come home with me and I'll show you," he said, pulling me tight against him.

"You're incorrigible."

He took my face once more and gave me his special kiss. We had made the decision to not sleep together the last month before the wedding, and our relationship was benefiting from a fresh degree of flirtatiousness.

What a whirlwind it had been. With the planning and arrangements of our upcoming vows and honeymoon, and the sale of my New York co-op, I'd taken an extended leave of absence from the law firm. An associate who was out of town for a month let me sublet her apartment, and somewhere in the mix I even inherited a Bed and Breakfast in a tiny town in Colorado. I'd done research on the mountain village where it was located, and hoped to talk Andrew into a side trip during our travels. It sounded romantic.

The past few years had been twelve-hour days with little down time, so this working vacation was a coveted time to unwind. I had turned my case files over to Andrew and could easily fill him in if he had questions. It sometimes surprised me that we'd been able to build a relationship, but our working proximity made it convenient, and he had been persistent.

"Good evening, Jordanna." He answered the phone in his distinctive, clipped voice. "Ready to come back to work?" I loved that my father always called me by my given name.

"Not a chance, but thanks for the offer," I said affectionately. "I'm calling to let you know I've cleared my schedule and turned everything over to Andrew. I brought him up-to-date on my caseload, so if you have questions, you can check with him."

"Are you sure he's up to the task?"

"You're not?" I was slightly surprised at his question.

"Oh, don't get me wrong. He seems competent enough, but he doesn't hold a candle to Jordanna Olivia. I trust your judgment, however, so if he's going to be my son-in-law, I'll commence showing him the inner sanctum of Whitman and Burke."

"I appreciate your vote of confidence. He's clever at handling my clients in a savvy and capable manner."

"That's never been a question, but I'll start giving him more responsibility. Don't be a stranger. Stop in when you're around. Maybe we can do lunch next week? Call Carol and set something up."

"Of course. Thank you, Father."

The early September air was brisk and added a degree of bounce to my step. I had a list of things I wanted to accomplish before I met Andrew for lunch. We were meeting a realtor afterwards to look at a Brooklyn Brownstone we were interested in purchasing. Finishing two errands, I was lighthearted with my newfound freedom as I entered the third store. The boutique was elegantly subdued and had been highly recommended. I wanted lingerie for our wedding night, and the garden-level provided just the right amount of light and privacy for intimate apparel shopping.

Coming out of the fitting room, I saw Andrew through the tinted window leaving the building across the street. Surprised and pleased to see him, I started to call out when I remembered my scanty attire. Hurrying to the dressing room, I grabbed my phone and headed back to the window to text him and let him know where I was. He turned just then toward the blonde woman who walked out behind him. Their lips almost touched, and I thought I was mistaken that it was Andrew, so I set down my phone.

He held her face in his hands and kissed her forehead, nose, and lips. The breath left my body. His arms embraced the fair-haired beauty who laid her head on his chest as he stroked her in the all-too-familiar way he had done to me so often. I tried to reactivate my brain to grasp what to do next.

Think, Jordan, think. Seconds passed before the adrenaline surged and I became somewhat coherent and focused. I grabbed a robe from a nearby hook and quietly opened the door. Magnifying my phone camera for a close up, I was able to capture several pictures of Andrew holding her face and kissing her before they slowly broke apart. I stepped back and let the door close, imagining it was closing on a huge part of my life.

Shocked as though hit by an electric current, I was still able to text to say something had come up and I wouldn't be able to meet, and asked him to cancel our appointment. Watching as he received the message, he immediately ran to catch up with the blonde. He put his arm around her as they walked away.

Was it possible I was mistaken? The photos told me the truth. I'd been kissed like that too many times to not understand that life as I knew it had been radically altered, and my world was going to be rocked to its foundation. It was all I could do to hold myself together. The clerk was sweet when I told her something had come up and I'd have to leave without purchasing her diaphanous creations. Alternating between disbelief and anger, I was unsure where to go, what to do. Was there protocol for something like this? The more I wandered, the angrier I got.

I wasn't aware of the miles I walked, but by the time I found myself in front of the advertising agency of my best friend, I was ready to detonate. How do you share this information? When does the trembling stop?

"What is it? What happened?" Jeni said, coming around the desk, taking me by the shoulders.

Too angry to be coherent, I pulled my phone from my purse and showed her the pictures. I saw awareness dawn, then indignation washed over her. "I was going to make excuses, think maybe you were wrong, maybe it's his cousin, maybe it's not him, but it's Andrew, isn't it?" she asked with fire in her eyes.

Nodding, I wanted to fling something. It unnerved me that I never saw it coming. I now understood the term 'blindsided.' A thousand questions, and they all came back to, "Was this my fault?"

"Don't you *dare* go there, Jordanna Olivia Whitman! This is *his* fault! You will not share an ounce of guilt, do you hear me?"

"It's not guilt, it's self doubt and anger and disbelief and stupidity in not seeing. What if I had *married* him? And the questions keep coming. How long has it been going on? Who is she? What did he want from me? But I can't seem to get away from, *How could I have been so stupid?*"

"You had no way of knowing. I can be done for the day. Let's get out of here."

As we headed down the elevator, she said, "What are you going to tell him? Surely you're calling off the wedding?"

"There's no way I can talk to him right now. I'm seeing red. And of *course* I'm calling off the wedding. I'm just not sure where to go now that I sold my co-op. How do you avoid the gigantic spotlight that'll find you when news like this breaks?"

"You can stay at my place. You know me, I'll put a favorable spin to it."

"I wouldn't think of putting you through something like that. God, Jeni, it's going to be awful."

"Jordan! Remember the letter you got last month about a Bed and Breakfast in some obscure little town? Where was that, Wyoming? Colorado? Did you ever respond?"

"People would think I was running away."

"Who gives a rip what anyone thinks? You've got lots of time off. You get to do what you want, especially right now."

"Having a drink sounds like a good option," I suggested hopefully.

"Sounds perfect. Come on."

We drank at several bars, but somewhere along the way I lost count of how many. I *was* aware, however, that with each successive stop, the funny side of today's surprise took hold. We were relaxed and silly by the time we got back to my temporary condo.

"I mean seriously, Jeni, what were the chances I'd be standing right there, right then? Kismet."

The familiar ding of Andrew's text came through. *Sorry you couldn't make it for lunch. I was so lonely without you. Want to meet for drinks?*

Can't make it. Out with Jeni. Will be in touch. Maybe you can find something else fun to do.

Nothing's fun without you.

I couldn't even respond. What a snake. How long had he been seeing her? It didn't look as though they'd just met.

"Wanna spend the night with me, Jeni? There's an extra room. My clothes fit you. In the morning we're either on the same page, or you'll talk me down from the cliff. Please?"

"We're diabolical plotters. Of course I will." We broke into laughter again.

"And you know what else?" I asked after a few minutes of silence. "I was excited about owning a Brownstone."

"Isn't *that* the truth? You might still want to, you just have to wait 'til the dust settles from *this* fallout before you think about taking a major step like that."

Lying on the couch a while later, she asked, "How do you feel? I'm ready to tear him limb from limb. What are *you* thinking?"

"Not a clue. The idea of going to Nederland has some appeal."

"Okay, but we don't decide anything 'til morning," Jeni said. "It's been a long day and your world derailed. We're not necessarily coherent, so let's see how you feel after a good night's sleep."

The morning dawned clear. Surprisingly, so did my brain. With Jeni's encouragement, I was warming to the idea of leaving town. "Not sure where the letter ended up in the confusion of my move, but I remember the name of the realtor that the lawyer mentioned I should contact in case I wanted to sell the place. I'll call her and get whatever details I need. In the meantime, we have to notify guests, figure out what to do with the gifts, the caterers, the travel arrangements, hotels . . . the plans."

I'd never considered myself vindictive, but I was ready to proceed. Jeni and I spent the day contacting caterers and venues and making the necessary arrangements to cancel a wedding that had been in the planning stages for months. Then we went to a print shop and waited while we had 'unvitations' printed, as Jeni was calling them. My marketing pal had done a great job designing them.

It was Saturday evening. I had a plane ticket to Denver for Monday noon. I made contact so I knew how to meet Callie Weston when I got there. I hadn't spoken with Andrew since the events of yesterday morning. What surprised me was I didn't feel sad about it. I was angry and embarrassed, but I didn't feel a loss yet. Time away would help me gain perspective. There was no part of me that felt a need to answer his calls. I returned his texts to tell him I was spending the weekend with Jeni attending to wedding matters and would contact him Monday, all of which was true. It's not like he was pining for me.

"I think it's poetic justice," Jeni said, "but I don't have as much at stake as you do. Sure you want to go through with this?"

"Telling my father will be the worst, but I'm sure he'll find a way to put the famous Wiley Riley twist on it. We both know how adept he is at that sort of thing."

"No question, he's the master. Okay, sweetheart, let's get these addressed."

Everything was in place by early Monday. Arrangements had been canceled and the unvites were ready for Jeni to drop in the mail. She was a trooper, staying with me the whole time, talking me through the ups and downs, helping me get the details done. Most important had been her encouragement that life was going to be deliciously different soon. I had one last stop to make before my flight.

Knowing he was at work, I used my key to let myself into Andrew's apartment. My purpose was twofold: to make sure I had all my belongings from his place, and to leave him a copy of the unvite so he'd have a clue of what was about to hit him.

Jeni and I discussed the pros and cons of giving him warning, but it was all the more appealing to think he would know beforehand and there wouldn't be a thing he could do to stop it. I had momentary twinges of doubt about whether or not to go through with it until I saw two wine glasses in the sink, one with a lipstick imprint. I had made the right decision. Much harder would be the phone call to my father during the cab ride.

As Jordan was landing at Denver International Airport, Andrew was arriving home after a tiring day. They hadn't spoken in a while, but he recognized her handwriting on the distinctive envelope on the counter. He immediately looked around, hoping nothing was out of place, and made a mental note to remember to be more careful in the future.

It was strange that her key was on the counter. "Jordan?" he called out. "You here?" He let out a sigh of relief as he reassured himself everything appeared to be in order · until he picked up the letter and noticed it was propped against two wine glasses, one with the betrayal of red lipstick on its rim. Tearing open the envelope, he saw the bold, perfect lettering that proclaimed: *LOVE IS BLIND*. He fell into a chair as he opened the card to see an intimate picture of him kissing Mary Ann with large letters announcing: *FORTUNATELY, I'M NOT*.

To order your copy of **THUNDER STRUCK** (Jordan and Brandan's story · Book 2 in the series) or **THUNDER SNOW** (Callie and Jack's story · Book 1 in the series) **visit Amazon.com**.

CURRENT BOOKS BY MIMI FOSTER

THUNDER SNOW – Contemporary – *Thunder on the Mountain* Book 1 – stand alone

Hiding peacefully for years in a remote mountain village, a well-respected but hardened businessman wants nothing to do with destructive emotional entanglements until a self-sufficient redhead invades his sanctuary and he must set aside his own painful past to protect her from the stalker who is determined to destroy her.

THUNDER STRUCK – Contemporary · *Thunder on the Mountain* Book 2 – stand alone

Betrayed New York lawyer escapes to a remote mountain town, but as she and a local contractor

endeavor to remodel an abandoned Victorian mansion she's inherited, they find journals from the past that are shockingly similar to the present as history begins repeating itself.

THUNDER STORM – Contemporary – *Thunder on the Mountain* Book 3 – stand alone

Determined to convince a captivating spitfire that short-term, long-distance relationships will never be part of his life, a Colorado contractor attempts to maintain emotional distance from a zany, enchanting New York ad exec as he keeps her apprised of the sometimes funny, sometimes poignant antics of her mentally-deteriorating grandmother who is being cared for in his remote mountain town.

JORDAN'S GIFT – Historical Novella – prequel to *Thunder on the Mountain* – stand alone

A hardened mine owner has little tolerance for people and enjoys life as a loner until he encounters a fiery newcomer who is running away from the conventions of high society and a broken engagement to his archrival. He will do anything to protect her from the smooth talking, black hearted, jilted fiancé as his nemesis attempts to destroy all he's ever worked for.

WILLOW'S SECRET – Historical – prequel to *Thunder on the Mountain* – stand alone

A capable and vibrant young woman works frantically to adapt to a swiftly changing world that threatens to destroy her way of life while the man who is bringing those inevitable transformations tries to protect the girl who has bewitched him and win her trust by teaching her she has the ability to control her own destiny and become a driving force in a male-dominated world.

MAISY'S MIRROR · Contemporary · non-series — stand alone

Healing from the car accident that killed her husband, the young author purchases a mysterious antique mirror and falls in love with the handsome reflection who tells her fascinating stories of daring and adventure and betrayal, but they know someday his illusion will not be enough to sustain their passion.

I love to hear from readers, so drop me a line at mimi@mimifoster.com or follow me on my website MimiFosterBooks.com.

If you enjoyed any of these books, please consider taking just a moment and giving a quick Amazon review. Thank you SO much!

Made in the USA
Lexington, KY
27 May 2017